Edwin Franklin Palmer

The Second Brigade

Camp Life

Edwin Franklin Palmer

The Second Brigade
Camp Life

ISBN/EAN: 9783337425210

Printed in Europe, USA, Canada, Australia, Japan

Cover: Foto ©Andreas Hilbeck / pixelio.de

More available books at **www.hansebooks.com**

THE
Second Brigade;
OR,
Camp Life.

BY A VOLUNTEER.

"TO KNOW
THAT, WHICH BEFORE US LIES IN DAILY LIFE,
IS THE PRIME WISDOM."—MILTON.

MONTPELIER:
PRINTED FOR THE AUTHOR BY E. P. WALTON.
1864.

PREFACE.

How the Nine Months' Men fared, that went from Vermont; how they felt; and what they did:—these it has been the intention of the writer to present; and, not to make any *one* man a hero, but to give Camp Life as he saw it.

With great diffidence, yet not without some hope of meeting the approval of his comrades, who endured privations so patiently, and fought so bravely for their country, does the author publish this little volume,—thinking that, when peace shall have been established, and the young men of the Second Brigade shall have grown venerable in age, possibly a perusal of these hastily written pages may revive some sweet (I hope not sad) memories of the camp and the field.

THE AUTHOR.

Waitsfield, Vt., December, 1863.

The Second Brigade; or, Camp Life.

CHAPTER I.

"From the gray sire, whose trembling hand
Could hardly buckle on his brand,
To the raw boy whose shaft and bow
Were yet scarce terror to the crow,
* * * * *
Each valley, each sequestered glen,
Mustered its little horde of men,
That met as torrents from the height
In highland dales their streams unite,
Still gathering, as they pour along
A voice more loud, a tide more strong,
Till at the rendezvous they stood
By hundreds, prompt for blows and blood."

WALTER SCOTT.

THE last day of September, 1862, the Thirteenth Vermont Regiment went into camp at Brattleboro'. The frost had come and turned the green leaves to a golden yellow, just so as to remind one that autumn was near by. The great battle of Antietam had just been fought, and high were the hopes of the people,—even that McClellan would force Lee rapidly back and capture Richmond. His army is so far North it must be annihilated, and hence the rebel capital captured.

Some in their enthusiasm fancied that we should never be ordered from the State. On the same day we received two blankets each; one made of hair, to throw around us when sleeping; the other of oil-cloth, to protect us from the storm. At six o'clock we ate. Our meal was made of wheat bread, cold beef and coffee. The first night our company had three candles, which, by cutting them into two or three pieces, lighted the barracks very well. The barracks are seventy-four by twenty-two feet, occupied by a hundred men. At half-past eight the roll is called; at nine the order is given—"No talking." This is not heeded. As soon as the officer retires, some show their skill by cackling like the rooster; others imitate feline, canine and taurine animals all at once. Bunks have been prepared to sleep on. These, made of planed boards, six and a half by four and a half feet, hold two soldiers each, and are two stories high. A little straw is brought to put in them; but it was our fortune to get none. So we made many turns during the night—first on one side, then on the other—"sweet sleep" not deigning to visit us.

Oct. 1.—The morning came foggy, drizzly. The boys spend the most of the day in making their barracks more comfortable—nailing narrow pieces of boards on the cracks. We succeeded in getting a little more straw; also a stove, just before night, by carrying it a mile on a wheel-barrow, through the mud and rain. The boys give three cheers for the stove, and the same number for those that got it. We are soon sitting around a good fire—some talking, some laughing, some smoking, others singing; all in good spirits. Our meals are made of wheat bread, cold beef, potatoes and coffee. Eight are detailed to act as guards, who are stationed around camp, and allow no soldier to go out unless he has a pass signed by his captain or colonel.

Oct. 2.—Rainy and foggy. No drilling through the day; but just before evening the clouds break away, and we had our first dress parade. It has been arranged that the companies may draw the raw materials and do their own cooking. Three cooks are appointed in each company, and they store away the fresh beef, bread, sugar, rice and beans in a shanty of rough boards. Four or five camp kettles have been furnished us for boiling coffee, meat, &c., and each soldier with a tin plate, cup, canteen, knife and fork. These form the soldier's culinary implements. After dark, I was attracted to the bright fires blazing by the side of each of the barracks. A ditch five or six feet long, two wide, one deep, is dug in the ground; wood thrown in; fires started, and the kettles steaming over these. The cooks are making their first attempts at cooking, who were as ignorant of the art as we of the military; neither knowing anything of either. The former, do doubt, had seen his mother boil beef and beans; we, in our childhood, had witnessed a June training.

Oct. 3. — Morning rainy. About nine o'clock the sun shines out. We drill awhile, and then draw our guns—the Springfield rifles, and gun equipments. In the afternoon, battalion drill. As fate would have it, my company, owing to some tardiness in the morning, is sent to clear the old camp ground of the Tenth and Eleventh Regiments. A meaner task was never imposed on Hercules. Filth! filth! rubbish of every description, and a mimic forest of pine to remove. Now you see a half dozen soldiers around one tree, lifting this way, that way—but it clings with great tenacity to the sandy earth. "By ——, I did'nt enlist to clear land for Uncle Sam," says one; they give it up; chop it down—drag it off; now the same number filling a sink—sweet work, I tell you; one is levelling the land with the spade; four or five are carrying off old boards; away on the plain the regiment is drilling for the first time with their bright rifles. In this way we toiled—some sweating, swearing, fuming, none in the best of humor—till near dark, when we returned; ate a meal of beans in the open air, and then turned into the barracks for the night—thinking that the sons of Mars had been insulted, to be set at such work. The next day was beautiful as the former ones had been stormy; and lovely as an autumn day can be. Company and battalion drill, dress parade, sweeping the barracks and the grounds about them with brush brooms made of pine, filled the slow passing hours.

Oct. 5.—First sabbath in camp. But how unlike a New England sabbath! No church bell do we hear; but "sonorous metal blowing martial sounds;" no neatly dressed people, winding their way to the chapel; but yonder weary sentinels, with the night's dew still glittering like pearls on the bright bayonets, are pacing to and fro: "Halt, halt," one cries; a soldier approaches, shows his pass, and out he goes. Here the cooks are cutting off beef, or dealing out beans to the boys as they come along by twos, and coffee, never colored by milk; anon the drum beats, and the sergeants start off with their men for guard-mounting. By ten o'clock comes "Sunday morning" inspection, hated by all the boys. This one throws down his pen: that one, his daily, or a testament that a pious sister gave him ere he started from home; a third has been dozing on his bunk; a fourth takes a long, hesitating suck at his fragrant pipe and carefully places it in one of his many pockets; but all hurriedly throw on their equipments, and with guns form the line, to be looked over by officers, for the most part, as ignorant as themselves of the etiquette of Mars. Straightway come religious services. All must attend.

The regiment forms a square; and to the soldiers, in various positions, standing, sitting, lying down, the chaplain expatiates on the temptations of those that go to the war. Now come a few hours rest, and then evening, the shadows lengthening eastward. On the thinly grassed plain in front of the barracks are many soldiers, strolling arm in arm. See them, different in mind as in form or feature. One, sad, shows me a letter, scarcely dry from the tears of his wife at home ; another, a fiery nature, tells over the Kansas forays ; the Nebraska iniquity ; the wrongs inflicted on Northern men : the firing on Fort Sumpter ; the great uprising in the North. "The Federal government is saved. Slavery is destroyed. McClellan will have annihilated Lee's army before we reach the field. The war will have been closed ere the sun shall make another circuit," he says. A few hours more, a third comes along, and laughing, "Have an an apple, Sergeant," and tells how he ran the guard, and "hooked the old man's fruit down by the river." Still a fourth, a sly one, has overheard the countersign, and so he gets out; but at nine the countersign is changed to catch the rogues ; and, "poor Jim, you are shut out, and the heavy dew on your coat and cap, the next morning, tells that you were poorly housed last night;" and away on the right (of the regiment) is a prayer meeting. Thus the day and evening went. The next was a busy, noisy day. Fifty men are detailed to work on the barracks, for a new regiment that came in after dark, amid cheers and martial music. There 's the usual drilling fore and afternoon; and wheat bread, cold beef and coffee—with now and then a change to rice or beans; and occasionally an old farmer makes us a visit with his milk cart, who always goes back with empty cans. Cadets—no doubt adepts—drilled the officers, and they, in turn, the next hour, disposed of their newly gained knowledge to the privates. The next two days are similar as to weather; or what we did, or ate; save on the first day we escorted one regiment out—and on the second, one into camp. The sun rises bright on the frostbitten forests, and the fields white with dewdrops. But ere Aurora scatters her pearls, the drums have broken the silence, and the sergeants are shouting to the top of their voices "Fall in! fall in, company." There is a stirring among the boys. They roll over; rub their sleepy eyes; start up; put on their coats and boots—those that do not sleep with them on;—stumble out of the barracks into line, and answer to their names. The day has commenced. The drum beats for sweeping the ground and barracks; for breakfast; for the sergeant to take the sick to the surgeon; for guard-mounting; for company drill; for dinner; for battalion drill; for dress parade, the evening meal, the roll-call at night; and tattoo, at half past eight, blows out the lights. The boys, rolled in their blankets, are lying in their straw bunks, and the day is ended. In the afternoon of the next day, we are inspected by the governor and adjutant general, with knapsacks, haversacks and all on, for the first time. Around we go, each carrying from thirty to fifty pounds—swaying this way and that way, especially as we wheel. One jogs his neighbor, and he his, the momentum increasing as the jogging passes along, till the left of the companies is quite broken. The knapsack don't hang quite easy. It is the first time. Now you see one of the weaker ones—his head half down to his knees—raising it higher on his shoulders; half are getting them in new positions. An old soldier that moves with such steadiness, though he has been through the same process, would smile and mutter "You'll lighten those knapsacks before you march far." But is it strange? The farmer is made lame the first day he mows. Can the scholar or merchant use the sickle or swing the scythe? Are they poor soldiers? I saw them nine months later moving steadier on Cemetery Hill amid a storm black with bursting shells to a place abandoned by an old regiment; I saw them a few hours later, when our thinned and shattered ranks were giving way, charge down the plain a hundred rods in front, and capture eight cannon from the foe; I saw them on the third of July, long ere the sun had risen, roused from sleeping on their guns, by hostile cannon, in the front line of battle, till nine o'clock at night, withstanding the furious onslaughts of the enemy, till they were rolled in frightful heaps, and not a man breathed in their front, that dared to flaunt a rebel flag in their faces, and now he, who looks upon the tattered banner they bore on that victorious day, may read "Gettysburg" inscribed for their signal bravery.

"Never was horde of tyrants met
With bloodier welcome—never yet
To patriot vengeance hath the sword
More terrible libations poured."

Oct. 10.—On the 10th we were mustered into the U. S. service, and save a few pugnacious sons of Erin, who are easily "persuaded" when they find themselves surrounded by a dozen huge, armed men from another company, all take the oath of allegiance cheerfully and enthusiastically.

Oct. 11.—The next morning, dark and cloudy. There is tumult all over camp. Soldiers are hurrying to and fro with more than common anxiety in their faces. Squads are here and there talking. You go into the barracks; the knapsacks are all packed; the haversacks filled with two days' rations—wheat bread and boiled beef. Citizens, fathers, mothers, brothers and sisters, who have come a long way, are there too. They have sober faces. They speak with trembling lips. They shed tears. They shake hands, and say "God be with you!" We are off to the South.

CHAPTER II.

Oct. 12.—If, indeed, it were necessary, to portray camp life, to describe the places through which a regiment passes, it is impossible for a soldier to do it, as night rarely puts an end to his travelling:

> "War and chase,
> Give little choice of resting place."

He but gets a glance of the spires and conspicuous objects in great cities, and the smaller towns fly from his memory as from his vision. He is no traveller in the popular sense of the word. He sees things as one the moon when broken clouds are flying by it—a view for a moment and it is gone. It is approaching noon. A long line of cars is lying near the depot and the engine is steaming up. Our friends had gone home in the morning. A few citizens had gathered around, and spake words of sympathy. But no, we want none; we need none; the mind is made up. "We are bound for Dixie," shout a dozen jolly fellows, as they ascend the car steps; "John Brown's knapsack is strapped upon his back," sing half the company; and the iron wheels begin to rattle, and the engine to scream. As we pass down the beautiful valley of the Connecticut river, the fishermen in their little boats take off their hats; the farmers in the fields, too, show their sweaty brows and raise their sickles: the women and children flutter their handkerchiefs from the windows and doors of the white cottages, and the boys are sure to return the compliment to smiling faces, by a wave of the hand from the car windows. The people of Northampton loaded us with the best of apples and cakes. We reach and leave New Haven, on a large steamer, a little before midnight, and at daybreak find ourselves at Jersey City. Though not half had ever been on the water before, after a little observation, sleep overcomes curiosity, nor stars, nor moon, nor splashing waves, or anything connected with the sea, nor thought of friends behind, were much to us.

OCT. 13.—The morning is cold and windy. Soup—"swill" soup,—and "slop" coffee, is furnished us in large barrels, I dare say, that never have been washed since Fort Sumpter was fired upon, at which my stomach at once revolted, and, though prodigal sure, I had not been from home long enough to "feed on the husks of swine," and so had recourse to the better contents of my haversack. By half past nine the cars are bearing us towards Philadelphia, and by the middle of the afternoon the discharge of a cannon announces our approach to the latter city. The people, as is their custom to all the regiments that pass through their city, gave us a good meal of wheat bread, butter, cheese, meat and coffee, and did us all the honor and every kindness in their power; and long after, when in the field, the boys often spake of the good people of this city and Northampton. It is Sabbath, and hundreds throng the streets at our departure. Although Antietam had been fought, hardly had they recovered from the excitement caused by the invasion of Lee, and anxiously were they looking for McClellan to pounce upon him in his retreat. The next morning, a little after two, we find ourselves winding the streets of Baltimore in a furious storm of rain. Here and there a pale light glimmers through the closed shutters, and though weary and sleepy, the firing on the Massachusetts soldiers occurs to our mind, and we almost find ourselves soliloquizing, "Won't they give us a similar welcome?" Morning comes to our no little delight. Bread, ham and coffee is our breakfast. Soon the dirty cars are slowly trundling on to the Capital, at which place, after many halts, we arrived the middle of the afternoon. Soldiers are strung along to guard the railroad from Baltimore to Washington. As the cars halt we look for the marble capitol; we see a long line of poor mules mounted by negroes, who are lashing them terribly, as I fancied *they* had been ere they were "contrabands;" we look again for the home of "Uncle Abe"—alas! that a numerous herd of swine rooting in the mud should meet our eyes. We give it up; follow the regiment to the barracks near the depot; throw off the knapsack; and, sitting on it, address a few short letters to our friends. Supper a little before dark, at the Soldier's Retreat—bread, raw ham and coffee. Before nine o'clock many a one has scribbled a line to his friends, at which time the lights are extinguished, and soon a thousand men are snoring side by side on the dirty floor. The next morning—no breakfast. A little before noon we are marched to our camp ground on East Capitol Hill; and here we remained, standing, lying on the ground, impatiently waiting, when we receive the shelter tents just before dark. These are made of cotton cloth, and five feet square. Each has one piece. Two, and sometimes four, are buttoned together; then suspended on three guns, in the centre, with the corners fastened to the ground with picket sticks. This is the airy dormitory of four, who lie in pairs—the feet of the first at the heads of the second. Meanwhile our faithful cooks have started fires and furnished us with coffee, and the commissary with bread.

Oct. 15. — Early the white tents disappear all over camp, as the guns are needed, blankets rolled and tied to the knapsacks. Brigade review in the afternoon—four regiments. As we march, counter-march and wheel over the broad plain—new work all—strange positions all—more than one mutters "This knapsack!" "Why carry it on this review?" "What good!" But it is ended. That's the best part of it. We return, eat a meal of beans, rear our tents in parallel rows, hang the rubber up at one end to break the wind off, light the candle, stick it in the bayonet and this in the ground, and pass the time as best we can till tattoo. General Orders No. 1 is read to each of the companies, making our duties similar to those before we left the State. At eight o'clock a prayer meeting.

Oct. 16.—Like the day before.

Oct. 17.—A lovely, autumn day; the air pure; the sky cloudless. In the forenoon squad and company drills: in the afternoon battalion. The A tents have been furnished us; much delighted to exchange them for the little ones. One, covering a little more than six feet square when pitched, is allowed five.

Oct. 18.—Five in one tent six feet square! We lie down on the same side, either right or left, parallel; as one turns all must. Most of the forenoon is spent in cleaning the grounds with spades, and brush brooms made of cedar. In the afternoon brigade review—six regiments and two Massachusetts batteries. Generals

Banks and Casey are present. You see many whispering in an undertone, "Which is he?" "Which is Banks?" As they ride by, in front and rear, many turn their heads, squinting over the shoulder to see them. When the review is over, we march to General Casey's head-quarters, on the opposite side of the city. The boys are tired, and think they have marched ten miles. We know nothing about marching in a brigade. We are now at a slow pace, now rapid, now running; here's one that's stubbed his toe and stumbled his whole length, causing laughter; there are several on the side-walk leaning against the posts: many are changing their guns from one shoulder to the other. I hear one expressing himself, with not a few gesticulations, in this wise: "I have a far less opinion of our Generals than before. Why all this? Is it for a show? Why is Lee suffered to escape uninjured? For eighteen months the war has proceeded, and how much have we gained? Richmond? No. The destruction of their armies? How long since they chased ours across the Potomac? I hear it whispered that we are going into winter quarters, to freeze in the barracks about

Washington. Why don't they send us to the old army, to spend our strength in conquering the rebels?" and many such. Others tell him that it is his part to obey, and not to command or criticise. But a Yankee, that has been a soldier only six weeks, has hardly lost his love for knowing the whys and wherefores.

Oct. 19.—Sabbath, warm, sunny. We are relieved from duties, so that we are reminded it is no week day. A refreshing breeze bears the mingling sounds of a dozen church bells from the city. How solemn! We forget our work, read a psalm, or some verses in the Testament, think of home and the tones of the old village church bell as they come up from the valley, to tell us of the hour of meeting.

Oct. 20.—The names of those that are to be guards are read off the night before. Last night my name was in the list. Morning came, and with it the various rounds of duties, reveille, roll-call, hanging up the things in the tents, policing the grounds, washing, breakfast, squad drill, then guard-mounting. A hundred and ten privates, six corporals, three sergeants, one lieutenant, have been detailed to guard the camp. This is their duty twenty-four hours.

They are divided into three reliefs, each on two hours, off four. None but privates walk the beats, which are from four to ten rods. The corporals run at their calls. Strange did it seem at first to be awake at midnight, hearing a half dozen screaming "corporal of the guard, No. 1," or 5, as it may be. Two large tents is the guard-house. As night grows darker and colder, the dew heavier, a whole relief, thirty-three, crowd into them, some standing, some lying parallel, others horizontal on the legs of the first tier. Towards midnight faces grow sober. "This is pretty raw," says one; "little tough," another: "one must be drunk or mad," continues a third, "to enlist." But as the sun returns, with it smiling faces and good feelings. "Soldiering is not very hard after all," say the same. "Not half as hard as I thought it," &c.

Till the 25th the history of one day is of the others. Camp quiet. At five, the drummers and fifers, whilst the stars still shine, march around camp, beating their drums. Sleep is frightened from every eye; a stir, a bustle in every tent. The boys creep out with their woolen night-caps on, and attend roll-call. Then some go back, wrap themselves in the blankets, and await the coming day; others laughing, talking, smoking, sit around the cook-stand, where the cooks are preparing breakfast, somewhat to the annoyance of the latter. The boys come along in two ranks, to get their food. Various remarks. This one would like a "little more variety;" that one "wouldn't look at it at home;" this one "don't fancy mule beef;" but most think it as good as the government can furnish, and approvingly point to the increase of their weight since they left home. Lately the dust has become almost intolerable. The wind plays with it as fine snow in the winter. As we go and return from the plain sometimes you cannot see the length of the company, thick clouds of dust filling the eyes, and each one looking like one that's threshing grain.—Whilst on Capitol Hill, five soldiers from each company are permitted to go to the city a day. On the 22d, after getting a pass signed by the captain, colonel and brigadier general, we started at ten to return at five P. M. for dress parade. The streets are patrolled by soldiers, but no one asked us for our pass. Two hours at the Patent Office; two hours at the Smithsonian Institute; a glance at the President's house; a stroll through the capacious Capitol. Who from reading the title of a book would essay the critique? nor will we to describe those places. But many soldiers are in the Capitol, who move about as if they were on their own farm.

I hear arguing in this wise: "We've as much right here as anybody; Abe Lincoln has no more. We are freeborn Americans, and have come here to defend our own property. It is now no use to ask 'Who caused the war?' But talk it as it is, both are to blame. The sun over the equator sends its rays not so obliquely as at the poles. This beautiful structure stands on the line between us and Dixie. Now when men come here, they should lean neither way. But, Tom, the South leaned a little the most—a little too much, and when we sought to make them go straight, they pushed us off and fired on our forts and stole our goods. There are little fishes in one of the caves of Kentucky, where the bright light of the sun never penetrates, that have no eyes, or even sockets for them. The Southern herd, and not a few in the North, are like them—

born and bred in the den of slavery, they know not what liberty is, and have no love for it. And as I look on these empty seats, and think how the politicians have inflamed them against us, I grow mad, madder even than in the fight, and wish them, if nothing worse, banished from the land. One thing we'll do, Tom, if we survive these troubles and ever turn our steps homeward. Not a man shall enter these halls, that loves not his whole country, who will not strike down Cæsar, or let Cæsar live, whichever will save Rome; that is, who will not strike down slavery or let slavery live, whichever will save the Republic."

Oct. 25.—Saturday, warm, dry, dust flying, and making everybody uncomfortable. In the forenoon battalion drill; the afternoon is for the soldier to wash himself and clothes. Accordingly we started, not with gun or spade, but the last week's shirt, towel and soap under the arm, and found a plenty of water, better than it looked, after wading out from the muddy bank of the Potomac. Two Irishmen expressed it about as it was, standing in as much mud as water: "By jabers, Jamie, this washin' I don't like." "In faith, no don't I, Pat, but the washin' is better than the varmin—and I catch two louse on me to-day."

OCT. 26.—It is the Sabbath, but no Sabbath to us. Last night one of the soldiers died, the first in our regiment. His body is sent home to his friends. Sadness came over all, longer than when deaths came more frequent. By eight o'clock it begins to rain. Soon the dry, mealy dust is laid, and the water is gathering in the lowest places. Now the boys, with have-locks and rubbers on, are creeping out of their tents, scrabbling after the spades and pickaxes, to turn the water from their little domains, on which it is beginning to encroach most ruth-lessly. It pours down all day. Just before night, I, with another one, start after some straw to lie on, as we have nothing but a few cedar boughs to sleep on, and these are very wet. We plod on through the mud till we come to a stack of cornstalks. The owner remonstrates: "My horse has nothing else to eat." "And we've nothing else to lie on." "But do you see I've not right smart of stalks?" "Do you see how the water is run-ning under our tents?" "I swear, I'm as loy-al a man as in New England, and my horse will starve." But he finally admitted that it is a hard case, gave us what we could carry, and would take nothing for it. But woe on the poor horse if the man told the truth; for when the boys saw us returning, it was as when a bee comes back to his cell, well laden from a piece of new-found honey; in a moment it is covered with the begging tribe. We spread the dry stalks over the bottom of the tent, the rubbers over these, and at nine lie down in a very comfortable condition. At one o'clock at night, the rain has not ceased at all and a chilly wind is howling among the swinging tents—a corporal comes to me with "Holloa there, you take the place of a sick man on guard!" Soon my boots, coat, rubber, havelock are on, and I start for the guard-house, where are thirty men in similar plight. A corporal posts us around camp, and for two hours we walk the beats, then we go back, throw off the out-side covering, and creep in by the side of some sleeping comrade. The next morning is cold and wet. Quite a number are sick. The cook stand is flooded, so we have no coffee. By ten the clouds break, spots of blue sky appear, to the no little delight of we wet fellows. The boys flock together in squads and tell over their fate. This one "was half covered with water when he awoke;" another "would have drowned, but his head laid on his knapsack."

The Sixteenth Regiment came into camp a little before dark, hungry. We divided our bread, beef and coffee with them. They knew it was the best we had, and cheered us as loud and hearty as if we had spread the viands of kings before them.

Oct. 28.—The usual round of duties.

Oct. 29.—In the afternoon the first lieutenant of my company died of typhoid fever. We are excused from all duties through the day. Suddenly and sadly his death falls upon us. We meet and vote to pay his expenses, and send his body home embalmed; and pass resolutions expressive of our grief; and tender our sympathies to his friends. At nine o'clock at night orders came that we must have our knapsacks packed, haversacks filled with two days' rations, and be ready to start at eight in the morning. Where are we going? This is the question.

CHAPTER III.

'Tis nine o'clock. The drum beats "to strike tents." The cotton city falls, unlike ancient Thebes, fabled to have risen at the sound of the lyre. At eleven we have just crossed the Long Bridge, and rest half an hour on the banks of the river. "Lay there, will you?" said the soldier by my side, as he hurriedly throws the stuffed knapsack on the ground, and casts revengeful looks upon it, as if the inanimate thing was conscious of what he was saying. And he intends that it shall be, for ere he has ceased berating "Uncle Sam's little trunk," he is sitting on it, and continually adding to his weight by devouring large pieces of bread and meat from his haversack, which is now on the ground between his feet. The half hour is soon up, and we start. For what place, and for what object? I don't know. A dozen have already asked me that question, and only one reply—"I don't know." In two hours we rest again, marching westerly. We continue our course, passing soldiers encamped here and there, earthworks and cannon, till about four o'clock, when we halt in a piece of woods, and the colonel begins to look for a good camp ground. The spot selected is a fine one, though covered with brush, surrounded on all sides with an oak forest save the one fronting the east. It is between two hills—quite romantic, and a pure stream of water runs through the little vale. The boys are soon clearing the grounds, as farmers in new countries, cutting, picking, burning brush. We had marched slow, and the teams were but little behind us, but we did not get our tents pitched, and pine brush cut to lie on, till after dark. There is no drilling the next day, but clearing the camp ground. All are well pleased with the situation and hope to remain for some time.

Nov. 1.—Early, orders came to be ready for brigade review. Accordingly we rub the rust from our guns, the dust from our clothes, and start at the appointed time. We have gone but a mile, when higher orders come for us to countermarch, return to camp and get ready for a move. As we reach camp, the colonel tells us to pack only such things as we actually need, and throw the rest away. The boys begin to ask, "Where are we going?" Some say this way and some that way. By noon the things are all packed, the sick cared for, the tents "struck," and we are off at a rapid pace. 'Tis hot as summer. The sweat runs down the red faces as rain. Two miles, thank heaven! and a rest, for I came near "giving out;" two miles more, and a second rest; two more, the sun is going down, and we are pitching our fly-tents, a mile south of Alexandria. Reports say the enemy are near. Two companies are sent out as pickets. The rest of us sleep finely till morning, with only the rubber between us and the ground.

Nov. 2.—Sabbath morning. How long we remain here, or where we are going, no one knows. The first thing, we start fires, boil coffee in our little cups, and eat breakfast. At nine o'clock we start again, and march a mile and a half through a hilly country, covered with underbrush, then halt and begin to clear the ground for encampment. The boys cut down the large trees; pull up the smaller;

scrape off the leaves, brush, and burn them. Just before we are ready to pitch the tents, orders came to "quit work and leave the ground." Of course the soldiers are not in the best of humor. To spend three hours work in cutting, pulling little trees, scraping the ground with bare hands, to get a place to lie on, and then leave it, is not much to the taste of a Yankee, who, when he works, would like to know the reason for it. "Why this?" "What next?" "For heaven's sake, where are we going?" "Does the general know, himself?" These queries rise in every mind, and some find vent. But in a short time the reason of this is known. The man, owning the land, wavering between loyalty and disloyalty, whose property is guarded by a Union soldier, ordered us off. But arrangements are soon made with the manor lord, and we remain.

Nov. 3.—We spend the day in pitching the A tents (the teams had not reached us the day before,) and policing the camp. Five companies are sent out three miles in advance as pickets; nine remained in camp. The next two days are about the same; no drilling, no reviews. Some are beginning to amuse themselves by whittling rings and pipes from the laurel root. On the 4th my company elected the third sergeant as lieutenant.

Nov. 6.—It begins to be evident what our work is to be, for a few days at least—picketing and building new forts around Alexandria. Five Vermont regiments form the brigade, and are encamped near each. One hundred and thirty are detailed from our regiment to work on Fort Lyon, large, and about half finished. We leave camp at seven in the morning, and start to return at four P. M. The men are busy during this time, with spades and pickaxes, save an hour at noon, when they ate four "hardtacks" each. We are digging a wide and deep ditch about the fort. The ground is so hard that none of it can be shovelled before picking. We remove five thousand eight hundred and thirty-two feet. We go back to camp feeling like day laborers; but the toil had sharpened our appetites, and never did epicure sit down to his chosen dish with such zest as we to our plate of beans and pork.

Nov. 7.—The morning is cold and windy. By eight o'clock it begins to snow, quite large and frequent drops. The soldiers are disappointed, not expecting it so early in the year, and then their tents are not fitted for it—no fires in them, except the commissioned officers'. They have small stoves carried on the wagons. Snow and sleet fall all day, and by night it is five inches deep. Soon the boys are stirring, to get fires in their tents some way; for they fairly shiver in them, and it is too stormy for drills, or work on the forts, or any duty save guard or picket, which knows no storms, no Sabbaths, no nights. Every soldier turns mason, and they make little fire-places out of stone or brick, which they have brought half a mile from an old camp ground, on their backs. They dig a channel under the tent, some three feet long; brick up the sides; cover these with flat stones or pieces of iron; and at the end for a chimney. Some of these worked finely; others smoked intolerably. Now you see the boys, tears streaming from their eyes, coming out of their tents, the smoke rolling after them. They get wood from the surrounding forest. Slowly the day wears away, but not a murmuring lip. Early the hospital, two large tents, where there is a fire and room for twenty-five or thirty soldiers, is crowded, and many a sick one shivers in his thin tent, through the door of which unwelcome snow is sifting. It freezes quite hard; but the sun returns fair, warm, and before night the snow has nearly disappeared. There is no drilling, as if we had suffered enough the day before.

Nov. 9.—Sabbath. No religious services, as the chaplain has gone home on account of his sick friends. The boys write home, almost an hundred letters going from each company; and nothing delights them more than to get an answer in return. War is barbarous, and thank heaven for the art of printing and writing, by which the thoughts of the dead are preserved, and distance is nothing, that we may converse with friends. For the solid granite is worn away by the dropping of water, and is it strange that the human soul is warped by constant exposure to the fires of evil?

Nov. 10, 11.—All are in doubt how long we remain here, though the colonel says that we have been ordered to build log huts for winter quarters as soon as we can get saws, hammers and a plenty of axes. But the great army under Burnside to the west of us, is advancing, and none believe we shall spend the winter here. It is now already known that McClellan is removed from his command. His admirers talk something in this way:—"How long will the administration pursue this vacillating course? How long will fanatical politicians be suffered to make and unmake our generals? Who has done so much as McClellan? has been so brave on the field, so wise in counsel, so deaf to faction, so true to his country? Who but he drove the enemy from Western Virginia? Who but he saved the Capital? Who but he forced the rebels back from Yorktown to Richmond? and what but the treason of McDowell, or the hellish intrigues of demagogues, prevented its capture?" And his opponents thus: "Saved the Capital! when he wouldn't go to Pope's rescue last August, as his shattered army was staggering back to Washington, from blows dealt by rebels that escaped from his own front. None done so much as he! when he left the foe where he found them? None so brave on the field! when he was never under fire? so wise in counsel! when he quarrelled with the venerable Scott? so deaf to faction! when his political friends are crying 'Peace'? so true to his country! when his country has lavished everything upon him, and he has done nothing in return. This is the humbug McClellan." These are the two extremes; but by far the greater part care, not so much who leads them, as that he, who does, shall lead them to victory.

To the 17th one day is like the other—for drills and little guarding; but all are busy, building the barracks. These are ninety-four by fifteen feet for each company. "A lodge of ample size." Each company builds its own, made of oak logs, which are plastered between with mud, and the covering is dirt. They are also banked up. There are several partitions in each, and in each room quite a large fireplace. They all run parallel with a street a rod wide. This is the plan, but slowly the work progresses, for we have but few axes; some chop down the trees; others split them, and still others draw them to the spot. On the 17th two hundred and fifty are detailed as pickets, to remain two days on the line. They start off with guns, equipments, blankets and haversacks. The camp is quite lonely, and there are a thousand rumors—a few more than usual.

Now we are going farther South; now a great battle is raging somewhere, sometimes we, and then the foe are routed; now our army will winter around Richmond, then it will go into winter quarters on the Potomac; now England will recognize the South at once: and finally the coming Congress will compromise the whole thing. They came back on the 19th, and whiled the afternoon away, in telling how they made their houses of cedar boughs; how they stopped every body unless they had a pass, and sent them back muttering; how this one chased a rebel cow, and filled his canteen with milk; how this one made a visit to a rebel hen-roost, and had a chicken for supper; and how Tom cried "Halt" three times in the dead of night, and "in a half second more would have fired his gun, when an old horse turned and showed the foe had four feet."

Nov. 20.—Last night we were ordered to be ready to start early for brigade review. Where? One says on Capitol Hill; another at Fairfax Seminary; and still a third and fourth have fixed on some place. It rains hard all night. The morning is wet and foggy; and there is mud in abundance. At eight we leave camp. Some of the boys have their breeches' legs tucked into their boots ; others have them rolled up five or six inches. Now we are about three miles from camp, having passed through Alexandria, a city of mud. "Halt," "countermarch," come the orders. The boys mutter : "this is putting down rebellion,"—a very current expression when they don't see things as some do that wear shoulder-straps. But the black skies hasten our steps, and we reach camp just in time to avoid a furious rain storm—boots and breeches covered with mud that sticks like paint.

To the 25th some work on the forts ; some on the barracks ; and of course each day at nine is guard-mounting. The regiments take turn in doing picket duty. Daily we get the mail. Doubt, as to our remaining here through the winter, is giving way, and love of the place is springing up in most minds ; for there is a stream of good water near by, and a plenty of wood.

CHAPTER IV.

Nov. 25.—It is eight o'clock at night—dark, pitchy dark, and raining fast. The guards, as usual, to and fro, are pacing the trodden beats. In each tent is a candle burning, and around it a little squad of soldiers, all busy: some telling their accustomed stories; some smoking; some at a game of cards; now a lively song entices laughter; one is reading, another writing to his friend, with portfolio on his knees; perchance some weary boy has fallen asleep,—none dreaming of marches. Just now the colonel calls the sergeant major: "Tell the captains that their men must be ready to start at a moment's notice, with gun, equipments, forty rounds of ammunition, blankets and rations for a day." Ah! now the quiet scene is shifted. See the hurry, the bustle. The blankets, spread on the bunks for night's repose, are rolled and tied to the well-filled knapsacks, and haversacks crowded with bread and pork. Then the boys come forward for the death-bearing cartridge,—many with some facetious remark: "Fun with the rebels I reckon." "We are good for 'em." The sick in the hospital, and a few in each company unable to do military duty, are left behind. A little before nine we start, in the best of spirits, but not with a quick step, for it is muddy, and so dark that one can scarce see his comrade before him. On we plod through mud and water—hitting now this one, now that one, and in turn hit by the same—halting once an hour for a few minutes, and each time some fall asleep and have to be shaken, as we start—until half past three, when we rest in a pine grove. First we stack guns and start fires; then some spread their shelter tents; others arrange sticks of wood and lie down on these. My bed unfortunately happens near a pile of wood, and as often as sleep deigns to approach my eyes, some fellow, whose fire has burned low, comes after fuel, in a not very ceremonious manner. Half asleep, half awake, turning from one side to the other,—the rain spattering in my face,—I lie there, occasionally, I fear not in the most pleasant manner, ordering off some one stumbling about my head. Sooner than we are rested, day returns, cold and wet. But we have good fires, and around each you see a squad of soldiers, from whose blue backs steam is evaporating ; not desponding, but laughing over the night's march ; eating bread and pork which they have roasted, not as the followers of Æneas, "Verubusque trementia figunt," but on peaked sticks.—Nearly all get a little taste of sweet sleep—aye sweet ; for sleep a soldier will, that has marched all night through mud or water.

At eight we begin the march again, ignorant of our destination, and continue it until noon, with several rests, when we halt in a pine grove, just south of Fairfax Court House. Here we made fires and ate our rations. Then some, weary with the night's and forenoon's marches, with the blankets over them, near the fires, fall into a gentle sleep. In two hours more we are off, and encamp near Fairfax Station, a third time in a pine grove. Here some pitch their tents, and others make little bough-houses of small pine trees and limbs. I, with fifteen comrades, pass the night in one of these. Poles are strung along from tree to tree ;

limbs, placed on the ground, lean against these, with a similar covering to break the wind off. In the middle is a large fire. Around this we gather, make coffee, roast pork and eat; then comes smoking, story-telling, and now a song. If one happens to be in want of anything to eat, another is always ready to divide with him. The fire is kept burning all night, one tending awhile and then another. Wrapped in our blankets we lie down, feet to the fire. At midnight you hear the clicking of axes. Boys, whose shins are too cold to sleep, are up re-kindling the fires that have gone out by the few hours neglect. The next morning at eight we continue the march, resting at noon long enough to boil coffee in our cups of wire bales; now up and down little hills, now through a forest of pine or oaks, till evening, when we bivouac on the rough banks of the Bull Run, near Union Mills. Three companies are sent forward as pickets and stationed along the stream. Here are a large number of earth works and barracks, built by the enemy, and abandoned by him, when McClellan moved the spring before. Some go into these rough dwellings, made of pine logs and mud, (there are places to build fires), and pass the night; others use the tents.

All around grass sprang up and grew most luxuriantly during the summer months, undisturbed by the soldiers of either side. Many gather this for beds, softer by far than coniferous twigs, with which the soldier commonly covers his bunk. The engine followed us to this point, which before had gone no farther south than Fairfax Station, after Pope's retreat the August before. During the next five days our baggage—large tents, camp kettles,—and such of the sick as are able to be moved, arrive. Two companies a day go on picket. The rest pass the time in stockading a little, and discussing the object and benefit of late moves, and of no moves, something like this: "Only one regiment of the brigade has followed us. That we are here alone, what injury to the enemy or benefit to us? What necessity of our starting in a furious storm of rain, at nine o'clock at night, to tramp here, unless forsooth to give us exercise? Sigel, with his Germans, is at the Court House,—back fifteen miles; Burnside, and even Lee, is northwest of us. There is no one to support us, and we can't hold this point a single moment. Indeed, does any one know by whose order, or why, we came here at all? Already it is rumored, and I say with truth, that we are going back to our old camp. This, no doubt, will be styled a 'strategic' move. If to wear out an army by useless marches, and do the enemy little injury, is strategy, certainly the past eighteen months have called forth the most wonderful generalship the world ever saw."

DEC. 3.—One company is on picket. Three regiments have encamped near us. Rumor is unusually busy. At one time we are to join Burnside; at another, to patrol the streets of Washington the coming winter; now, go with Banks to Texas; then, into winter quarters at our old camp. A few spread these reports. and none believe them.

The next morning, I, with my company, start for the picket line along the river. This famous stream, like some men, had it not been for events that have transpired around it, would hardly have found place in print. The sterile bluffs, running to all points of the compass; rocky, so rough that you can hardly pull yourself up, carrying a gun; covered with scrubby oaks; pines and laurel with its green, orange-like leaves, in places, come down so near the turbid river, that the cheerful sun is invisible to us, save from half past nine till half past two in the afternoon. So winding and broken are the banks that often the pickets cannot see each other, whose beats are not more than twenty-five rods apart. Travel the stream for miles, and rarely is the diameter of the visual circle equal to a half mile.

It is a bright, frosty morning, little crystals hanging from every limb. During the night, for several feet, ice gathered along the shores. Here it is from five to ten rods wide, and fordable in many places. Wild grapes grow in profusion along the shores, which we thought a great luxury. Two or three are left at a post, and take turns in keeping watch. They have as good a fire during the day as they choose to build; but a small one by night, that cannot be seen far. Back sixty or seventy rods, in a thick pine forest, is the reserve, which relieves those posted in the morning.

It is Thanksgiving in our native State, and we had long anticipated a pleasant time: for our kind friends at home had sent forward boxes well filled with things edible, as good as any epicure could desire. These failed to reach us, so we ate hard tack and pork, and only laughed at our misfortune. Some, however, lament that they are not at home to enjoy the day. Memory takes along with herself a pleasing train—and not least to the soldier's heart—but as the fair, lovely forms are contrasted with present scenes, not so pleasing as the past, they do excite mournful emotions in many a bosom.

> "We spake of many a vanished scene,
> Of what we once had thought and said,
> Of what had been, and might have been,
> And who has changed and who was dead."

The school with its sweet remembrance, the church with its solemnity, the light dance, the love and bridal scene, and the reassembling under the paternal roof on this anniversary; all, or each, are topics for this, or that one, according to the bent of mind.

Fog, rising from the valley in the morning, passes over little hills, bends up, and soon is flying through the jagged notches of the mountain, if these are not too high, and then drop by drop, on leaf and moss, it loses itself. So some men with circumstances, according as they are rough and difficult, go, some over, round some, are lost in some; others, with steel-pointed drill and powder, start at once to cutting a road through the mountain. Here are a dozen good fellows, who have adopted the Lacedemonian code: "Steal (from Dixie), but not get found out," who are not to be bluffed out of a choice supper, by the mere circumstance of a few miles' march. And, so they—as they say—"Lay in a requisition in the name of Uncle Sam," with rifle in hand, scour the country around, and at night sit down to their tables of "hard tack" boxes, covered with chickens or turkey, or fresh pork.

CHAPTER V.

DEC. 5.—At ten o'clock every thing is ready to start. Soldiers, with their guns, equipments, knapsacks, haversacks and canteens; boxes of cooking utensils, stoves, spades, pick-axes, officer's valises, waiters, horses, tents, and every thing belonging to a regiment of a thousand men, are piled on to some flat-bottom cars. A few covered cars, with no seats, such as drovers use in New England, to take their herds to market, are hitched to the former, for the weakest ones, as the march to Bull Run has made quite a number sick. Just before leaving this rough place, which is covered with the ruins of burned cars, and where you are told that the left wing of our army rested in the first Bull Run battle, it begins to snow and rain. The cars move slowly over the military road, halting sometimes for half an hour—bearing their motley load. At four P. M., within about a mile of Alexandria, the boys are jumping off, wet to the skin, covered with snow and soot, as the wind was right to carry it back from the engine. We now start for our old camp, which we so suddenly left on the night of the 25th ult., and a little before dark, come in sight of the half-finished barracks. Every thing is wet, the ground is covered with moist snow—and more is coming; not an axe to chop wood for a fire; not a tent to spread, (these had been left at the depot with the expectation that they would be brought forward by government teams, but these could not be procured;) the boys hungry, and but little to eat. "What shall we do?" good-naturedly enquired Uncle Walter. "No where to lie, and nothing to eat." "Good that the old women at home don't know how we are; for the knowing it should give our friends more misery than we tough fellows who face the storm." "Now here's a proverb," responds Jack, who at one time is wont to distort passages of scripture; at another he is improvising poetry; now he is a sage, uttering wise sayings, or preacher, terrible denunciations against the wicked; again he is general, in deep meditation, plotting against the enemy;

all feigned, but with all, his good nature, and common sense too, make him a friend of each soldier. "Now here's a proverb that ought to make King Solomon and Ben Franklin blush: A place to lie on, a fire to warm your skins by, and enough to eat, are to be preferred to 'great riches' or a good name. And, that you need not think me less a general than a philosopher, let me plan a little for you. There's a negro's shanty yonder. Some of you lay there; and hard by is old Johnson's house and barn—some lay there—(yes, an old rebel he is too. Cuss on his head; if I was general, he shouldn't live longer than he could by hanging in a noose, higher than a pigeon could fly in nine months); yonder is a clump of pines—some lay there; and some of us will 'freeze' to our brothers in the other regiments. Now let me close with this sentiment: Let not a man despair; for a brighter sun will rise to-morrow, and our tents too; and in coming years, when your hairs have grown grayer than a rat a hundred years old, you, and you unmarried youths that never more than *threw* kisses across the school house to some bright eyed girl, will pass your peaceful nights in telling your grand children of your wondrous deeds in Virginny." Though Jack's words caused less merriment than when the boys were in better spirits, he had named the best places for us to pass the night. But there is little time to debate what is best. Each man must stir and take care of himself. Soon the whole regiment is scattered, except a few that hang around the dismal site of the old camp all night. As many as can, crowd into the negro's shanty, and his master's house and barn, and lie on the floor; the pine trees shelter a few; and quite a number are kept by the other regiments of the brigade. I, with twenty of my company, go to the twelfth regiment. Col. Blunt kindly gave us two large tents, where is a stove, wood, and a fire already kindled. As we enter, the boys chilly, with chattering teeth, say, "Bully for our Lieutenant; he cares for us." The officer then takes six of those who have suffered most from the storm, and calls on Capt. Cole, his friend in college. This regiment had got their barracks finished. The Captain goes to the cook shanty, raps on the door, makes known his errand. The chief cook, a fat, middle aged man, loudly replies:

"Let them in; we haven't denied a soldier to-night. Let them in: we will lie in the storm ourselves sooner than they. Come in, boys, come in," cries the cook, as though he meant they should. "We ha'n't all the accommodations, as if my wife was here; but we've a rousing fire, and you can lay on the ground." Such is the case. Logs a foot through and four feet long, with smaller wood, are burning lustily in the large fire-place—a most cheerful sight, more so on account of the cold storm without. Never was hospitality more freely given by knights or king in royal palace, or more thankfully received, than in that rough shanty in the woods of Virginia. The next morning many are fed by the other regiments. Col. Veazey gave me thirty loaves of bread. With these under my arm, I start for the camp, half a mile away, where we had left our guns and knapsacks the night before, and where all are to collect. On these the company breakfast. The storm has ceased; the snow is melting under a warm sun; but the camp ground repels one from it. It looks not unlike a field of ruins,—a stack of low chimnies here; a pile of logs there; hard tack boxes, pork barrels, bunks, some covered with straw, some with browse, some partly torn down. But by ten o'clock the tents are on the ground, and before night are all up on the old sites, cleaned as best we could. The boxes, containing our Thanksgiving supper, arrive; and, reader, I need scarce tell you that hard tack and pork does not form the supper; or, if curiosity prompts you to call into our little mansion six feet square, the roofs of which come down to the ground, you would doubtless be invited to take a seat on the wood pile. You might at first be a little surprised at the simplicity and disarrangement of our furniture; but we should make no apologies; for we are quite as well off as any of our neighbors, and that you know is enough the world over. There are our guns tied to the tent post, that they may not rust, (it is not a small job to scour them bright for inspection after being out in such a storm as we've had;) our equipments are under the bunk with knapsacks, haversacks and canteens; these cups, plates and knives, we also put in with them; but if we remain here a few days, we shall probably get a hard tack box, which will make us a fine cupboard.

And, too, this floor is not wholly without its virtue; for as a miller wears a white coat because it will not show the flour so quick as a black one, so our floor is good about not showing dirt, and we don't have to sweep it more than once a week or so. We six live in this tent very finely—a good one it is, never leaking unless it rains furiously; three of us old school mates; four of us republicans, one an abolitionist and one a war democrat. So we never have occasion to quarrel, only differing a little as to the slowness or swiftness of Mr. Lincoln in beating the rebels; not caring whether he does it by white men, or niggers, or by both. With few exceptions, we get enough to eat—always plenty in camp—not mince and chicken pies, of course, like that you see in the box: but wheat bread, pork, beef and beans, and rice twice or three times a week. And we have just guard and picket duty enough, with now and then an excursion, to keep up a good circulation of the blood. And now, reader, if you doubt our word, when we say that this is a most agreeable way of living, we can only advise you to try it.

Dec. 7, 8, 9, 10, 11.—Sabbath—cold, no religious services, dull. The boys stick to their tents—hardly out of them all day. The next three days we pass in completing the barracks, alternating in our opinions between going, and not going, into winter quarters here. A part build log houses and cover them with dirt—a few with oak slabs, split out with the axes; a part stockade the tents. On the 11th all that are able go on picket. The line is three miles south of the camp. It extends from a creek of the Potomac west for many a mile—our brigade keeping up the line for a few miles and then met by other soldiers. There are three reliefs; each on duty eight hours. The beats are from ten to fifteen rods apart: two soldiers are left at each, one watching at a time. They are each allowed such a fire as they choose to build night and day, as the enemy are not thought near. Our letters are brought us from camp just before dark. Of course we have no candles, so we punch the fire-brands together, pile on as dry wood as we can get, not sparing the rail fence near by. When it is well burning, we, sitting cross legged on the ground, leaning towards the fire, learn the news from home. The day is warm and so beautiful that one, little by little, almost forgets his native hills, and for the time, wishes to make the sunny land his home. But no, no,—ye native hills and rivers and lakes, we can never forget you. Thrice lovely and dear to us are ye in the distance. But even when we lived among you, so much to our taste and liking wert thou, that though we had looked upon thy varied forms from tenderest childhood, there was no satiety. Our love for thee grows stronger with the circling years, as grape-vines around the sugar-bearing maples. The next morning we are relieved so as to reach camp at eleven. On our way back we are told that Gen. Banks had taken Richmond, going up the James river with the gunboats; that several of the States had accepted the President's offer to buy the slaves. Quite a number think it probable, as the news comes from so good a source; others say that "it is too good to be believed;" but the faces of all look as men's are wont to, when they have suddenly heard good reports. All, as usual, do but little during the rest of the day, after being on picket. But all go out to dress parade.

It is closed. The men are beginning to leave the ground. Just now one of Gen. Stoughton's aids rides up, and hands the colonel a letter. He reads it; then (as is his custom) begins to bite his mustache, and rub his chin with his forefinger. Immediately it is noised through camp that we are to start on a march at five o'clock the next morning, with two days' rations.

CHAPTER VI.

Long before daylight the stars are shining brightly, and the camps are all alive. Things are being packed up: breakfast ate; such of the sick as are unable to march a part of the way and be carried a part on the ambulances, turned over to the regimental hospital, and thence to some general hospital in Alexandria or Washington; last, the tents are struck and loaded on the wagons, and we are off. The whole brigade is moving, commanded by Gen. Stoughton. This one declares that we are going up the Potomac; that one, down; this one, to Bull Run again; and that one, to Centreville. But if either is right, it is because he happens to guess it; for rarely does a soldier know long before, when, or where he is to march; and as well might one, unlearned in astronomy, conjecture the shiftings of the winds and storms, for the next generation, as for a soldier in the morning to pretend where he will be at night. They know this, submit to it, with little or no murmuring, and as soon as they halt for the night go to making them as good a place to lie on as they can. We have marched about a mile, when the sun rises above the low, wooded hills of Maryland, its rays flashing on the burnished rifles, and the long line of men rolling steadily over little swells of land, now seen, and now the living chain is broken from your view by the uneven land, looking not unlike a beautiful river, as seen from some neighboring hill in early day, whose silvery waters are winding through the valley below, at one time hid by rocks or strips of trees, and then pouring on, narrowing, till lost far away; so looked this line of brave men, each gathering courage as he sees the host stepping by martial music, and pride, that he, with such, are the defenders of his country. At ten we are told that Burnside has taken Fredericksburg; that soldiers have been pushed on from Centreville to support him; and that we are to occupy their places. A glorious day it is; a bright sun, pure air, just cool enough for exercising, and never did men march with higher spirits, all except the weakly; victory perching on our banners: and many, forgetful of the peninsular disaster, and the famous retreat of Pope, almost with their heated imaginations behold Richmond in flames, Lee, Longstreet and Stonewall Jackson in the old capitol prison, and the rebel army scattered like autumn leaves. My company is placed in the rear of all to pick up the stragglers, that is, such as fall out from their places. The teams, four horses to each, drawing large, heavily ironed, four-wheeled wagons—covered with coarse cotton cloth—of the whole brigade, start between us and the last regiment. There are seven for each, except our own regiment, and two ambulances, one drawn by four, and the other by two horses. Our teams had been turned over to the government when at Bull Run, and we had not succeeded in getting others, only for the ambulances. There are men in every company, who are just recovering from sickness, or just growing sick, or weak from diarrhœa—a most common complaint among the soldiers—or low from various causes, who prefer to try the march to being left behind, and hence sent to a general hospital. So they start with the rest.

We have gone a mile and a half. I now see one, pale, breathing hard and coughing; two comrades step along to him: "Johnnie, let us carry your knapsack;" a third comes up: "and let me have your gun." He goes on a mile or so; takes his own things; on again, till his strength gives out. Then some one assists him to get on the ambulance, if this is not already full; if so, then try the wagons. But what if these are loaded with tents, pork and hard tack? Then he must sit by the roadside till the rear guard salutes him. "Fall in, boys, fall in! We have orders to pass by none." He looks as though doubting whether to try the march, or not. But he slowly puts on his burden, and continues along with us for awhile. Now the whole brigade halts; and perhaps some ambulance which has been emptied of its soldiers, who have become rested, comes back to the rear, and takes those who have suffered most from the march. In this way there were not more than twenty-five from the whole brigade with the rear guard, as we reached the place of encampment, a mile northwest of Fairfax Court House, just dark, about an hour later than the main force. We have marched twenty miles. I saw only one throw his knapsack away—remember in this is everything a soldier has to keep him warm, and that he cannot long endure these frosty nights without his blanket,—and a surgeon got this one on an ambulance. We camp in the edge of a forest of oak and chestnut; here, instead of the open plain, as the leaves will be between the rubber blankets and the ground, and wood for our fires nearer. Most pitch their shelter tents; a few have lost them, and lie around the fires—I so near one that my overcoat receives a good scorching. Short is the time between boiling coffee, and lying on the leaves under the blankets; and still shorter between this and sleep. Early the next morning everything is arranged to continue the march. But the forenoon passes off, we expecting each hour to go the next; but in the afternoon it is understood that we remain through the night, and so we have a battalion drill. From one till dark, infantry, cavalry and teams, are marching by us to reinforce Burnside.

DEC. 14.—Sunday morning—calm and still save the tramp, the ceaseless tramp of cavalry and infantry that are rolling by us from early dawn till late in the evening. As one for the first time looks on the waves and tidal motions of the ocean, at once does he exclaim, "What power! how great, how grand, how majestic, is the ocean;" and if he dwells in the city, in ecstacy will he ride over the country, and breathe the pure mountain air: and in turn, a countryman's curiosity is not a little aroused by a stroll through the most ordinary city. But though the objects of nature and art are grand and beautiful, and great to stir one's feelings within him—all pale away, like stars before the silver flood of the morning sun, as he gazes long on the vast human sea, in a few hours to be thrown into fury by the shock of battle. Onward, onward they go, unbroken as a stream, and resistless as the tide, think we. "They conquered the rebels at Antietam: Burnside has again at Fredericksburg; he must capture Richmond this time," many say. Give the soldiers a plenty to eat; give them a general who will lead them to victory; pay them when they are in need, and rarely will you hear a murmur or see a better feeling set of fellows.

We have the usual Sunday morning inspection. The captains examine the arms to see that they are in good condition; and cartridge boxes, that there are forty rounds of ammunition. The boys spend not a little time in scouring and oiling their guns. For this purpose each has a little bottle of oil and piece of emery paper, which they buy of the sutler; or if wanting this, they use the top of the ground, soft, fine, a little gritty, but not so as to scratch the barrel. After the inspection is over, the colonel forms the regiment into a square and speaks as follows: "Soldiers, this inspection has been very imperfect on my part. But do not think there will be any relaxation. I ordered you to leave your knapsacks in your tents on account of this sudden march, thinking that your clothes might not be clean and well arranged. Now the object of this inspection is not to *make* your clothes clean, and guns bright, but to *know* that they are so. I see, boys, that some of you are getting somewhat dirty, greasy even, about the neck. There will always be a few in every regiment who don't have a care for these things. So they get vermin on them, and that isn't the worst;

necessarily they give the prolific creatures to others, who are very particular as to cleanliness. These things must be attended to:—your guns in good order, your clothes and persons clean. And since you have a little leisure, and there is a stream of running water near, and the day is warm, I advise you to do this as soon as you are dismissed; for you know you cannot on the march, and to-morrow you may be following in the steps of yonder veterans."

Many heed the colonel's advice and give their bodies a good scrubbing with soap and water,—most from inclination; but possibly a few, through fear of becoming unpopular with their comrades. Many hang out their clothes to dry, as they washed them the day before we started on the march; and so were packed into the knapsack wet.

Dec. 15.—Still lying in the woods; and still expecting each hour to start the next. Many rumors reach us from Burnside. Alas! his star, that shone with such splendor but yesterday, is shooting from the heavens with the comet's speed, scarce leaving one ray of light, —darkness closing in upon its course, like waters in the wake of a ship. Now he is shelling the city, and throwing pontoon bridges across the river; now his men are over, and Fredericksburg burned to the ground; now the rebels are flying back to Richmond, pursued by our victorious army. All are jubilant. But in a half hour more the news is brought us from Gen'l. Sigel's head-quarters at Fairfax Court House: "Gen. Burnside's whole army is driven back across the river with fearful loss." Never were bright skies so suddenly darkened by clouds; never did thermometer so frequently rise and fall by shifting storms, as did our spirits by alternate reports of victory and defeat. But just at night the surgeon comes into camp with a paper. According to this, our forces have been partially successful,—room for hope, but bitter comparisons drawn between Burnside and McClellan. We have had most fortunately three warm and pleasant days, but at four the next morning we are roused from sound sleep by rain coming through our shelter tents, as if made of paper. Soon all are up, stumbling around in the woods and dark, to start fires and throw the rubber blankets over tents. We are now short of rations. A few frequently have complained that they did not have what they wanted to eat; did not get what government furnished; but most have had a plenty until now. But last night, few ate more than half a meal, and now only six hardtacks for the day,—no meat, no coffee, no sugar, (deprived of either, a soldier is somewhat out of humor,) all expecting a great rain storm. There is considerable murmuring. Some of the rash ones, not to officers, of course, but to sympathizers, give vent to their passions thus: "I won't lift a hand until I have had more to eat." "I will help myself to the bread, and they can put me in the guard-house as quick as they please." As fifteen or twenty stand around a heap of wet brush, smoking more than burning, one rough fellow explodes in this way: "This whole war is a d—d swindling concern. It's kept up by infernal scoundrels to make money. Six hundred million dollars squandered in a year, and we half fed! Down here it is first nigger, then mule, and last soldier. We haven't drawn half our rations since we left home; but by the ——, I'll not stir another inch till they get us what we want to eat. When my time is out, if they get me again, they will get me by drafting. What a shame for a soldier to starve within four miles of a railroad, and in sight of Washington." Another answers, who utters the opinions of most: "We are now, and have been in the past, occasionally short of rations. But have we never gone without a meal when at home? And who thought of whining like a child? Didn't we suddenly start on a march, and hence the commissary was more or less disarranged? And to talk of starving as we now live, is merely talking. Don't we all weigh more than when we left home? Is this starving? Those, who will *eat* themselves sick in a week's time,—if the sutler don't get all his green backs before—of course will complain here. Didn't seventy-five thousand soldiers pass through here yesterday and the day before? All these must be fed. Let us look at these things like men. The wonder is, that the government feeds so many so well. The skies are dark this morning; and if Burnside is beaten, darker still our national affairs; not from the blow received from the rebels; but the traitors in the North will seize on this, and cry 'Peace.' It is time to *deplore* the event when we know the worst; but never to *despair*, whatever disaster befall our country."

Our A tents were brought by railroad to Fairfax Station last night; those of the rest of the brigade were on the teams that came with us. About nine o'clock quite a number from each company go down to bring them up on their backs,—four miles from the camp. As they plod on, the red mud sticking to their boots, they speculate thus: "Now if Burnside beats the rebels at Fredericksburgh, and forces them back to Richmond, we shall be ordered on at once to take their places on the Rappahannock; if he is driven back, we shall go to aid him. Hence, whichever way the tide of battle turns, we cannot remain there more than a day or two. So why carry these tents four miles on our backs through this infernal mud?" But after they have become warmed by exercising, all conclude that it is better to move about than to shiver in camp. Whilst at the Station, an old woman, whose dress was certainly never worn out by being washed, gets up a brisk trade with the boys, by selling pies,—some made of dried peaches, some of wild rabbit. We reach camp, and have our tents up before dark, in much better spirits than in the morning. Near by had been all day a pile of bread,—a thousand loaves. Around it a guard paces, shifting his gun from shoulder to shoulder. The soldiers think it ought to be dealt out. After dark (we are told) one creeps up slyly, seizes a loaf, and starts off on the run. Tne guard don't see him till off a number of rods. He now comes to his accustomed sharpness at once, and is on the thief's track, screaming "corporal of the guard! corporal of the guard!" Whilst on the pursuit, and before the corporal reaches the spot, another helps himself. In this way the pile was some smaller the next morning.

Dec. 17.—No drilling. Similar rations are dealt out as at the other camp,—soft bread, pork, coffee and sugar. Rumors of Burnside's defeat; grumbling in the North.

Dec. 18.—All of our things reach us to-day. Two men from a company were left behind to take care of them. The day after we left, Captain White died of typhoid fever. All are anxious (asking this one, and that one, if he has heard from Burnside,) to get an accurate report of the great battle at Fredericksburgh.

Rarely do daily papers come to us, though we get our mail every other day.

Dec. 19.—Lying in the woods; no drilling. The Colonel won't let us stockade the tents, as he says we shan't remain here but a short time. But few have any fires in them. The nights are cold. This morning, when I went to the little stream to wash me, I found it frozen an inch deep. If you wake any hour of the night, you hear the strokes of a dozen axes; and what is really painful, many coughing—coughing—deep and hoarse. The cold has crept through the tent and blanket, and thief-like, robbed the soldier of his sleep. He starts up, cold all over, feet, hands, head and body. His fire outside his tent has burned low. He throws the brands together, and then starts with his axe after wood. Now the logs are burning brightly, forming a beautiful circle of light, the radius of which is growing fainter and fainter till lost in the darkness; within is another circle of soldiers chatting around the fire. In the afternoon the bugle calls the officers about the Colonel's tent. The order is given to have their men ready to start at a moment's notice. This is soon changed, and we go on battalion drill. It has been rumored all day that McClellan is reinstated in power. At nine o'clock at night orders came from the brigade head-quarters for the whole regiment to go on picket the next day.

CHAPTER VII.

The sun's rays are glancing obliquely on the white frosty earth, as we start for the picket line, two miles south of Centreville, and eight from camp. The whole brigade is stationed near the Court House, and the regiments take turn in doing the picket duty,—each on four days. The rest of the time is mostly consumed in brigade and battalion drill, and keeping guard. We pass over the broad turnpike between the two villages—since 1861, now held by friend and now by foe—not level, but rising and falling, like waves one behind another. We have reached the summit of a ridge, running east and west—the highest point for a number of miles. On this is a long line of rifle pits, between works thrown up for cannon. A few rods south is Centreville, a village of twelve or fifteen houses that have been whitewashed sometime, with huge stone chimneys at both ends; occupied by negroes and government stores, as a few hundred cavalry have been encamped here for awhile, also doing picket duty. Far and near are barracks and ruins of barracks, built and occupied by the enemy in the winter of 1861, and abandoned by them in the spring of 1862. We know that we are on historic ground. Eagerly the eye siezes on objects to the south, glancing down the sloping hill, then on, over a wide tract streaked with forests, and cut up with little streams—still on five or six miles to Bull Run battle-field. Two companies are posted as pickets; the rest go into the filthy log huts. When new they were doubtless quite warm and comfortable; but now, parts of them are torn down, the mud out of the crevices, so that one is in doubt whether to take them or the open fields swept by cold winds. Water freezes in the canteens. Towards evening we get in some wood to burn, boards to lie on, hang the rubbers and small tents around the rough walls, and prepare for supper. A few stroll off and find places that they regard better; but the Colonel soon orders them back, saying that they were liable to be attacked by rebel cavalry during the night. A long dull night it is—too cold for much sleep.

DEC. 21.—Early, ten men and a lieutenant are sent out from three companies each, to act with the cavalry patrols, on the main roads—two miles from the village. Two are left on the beat, who are relieved once in two hours. The rest of us selected a place a hundred rods in the rear, out of sight as much as possible, in some wild rose bushes. These we clear away with our knives; start a fire; hang up pieces of shelter tents to break the wind off—nothing over us; gather hay to lie on, and we are rigged for the twenty-four hours. We have ten hard tacks each,—twelve is a day's ration—a little pork, coffee and sugar. Some cook—fry the meat by converting the tin plates into frying pans—sticking small sticks to them and holding them over the fire. The hard tack, soaked in cold water, is then fried in the lard. Some, however, eat it clear, now and then taking a draught of hot coffee. The cavalry patrols say that they are driven in, but we see no signs of the enemy. They had been in the war from its commencement, and were fond of relating their daring exploits;

how this one escaped at dead of night, with many balls through his clothes; how that one charged in first and second Bull Run battles; how from yonder peaks you could see dead men all around; and no end was there to their stealing the hens and pigs of "secesh" citizens. With us is a jolly son of Erin. He is a little blind and quite excitable. In the distance he sees a rebel in every old stump or rail fence; here they are pushing on towards us in four files; yonder are cavalry plotting against us: "That house up there is full of the divils. By jabers," says he, "we ought to burn it." When asleep, he dreams of battles, and making terrible charges on the foe:

"In broken dreams the image rose
Of varied perils, pains and woes."

It is the custom to halt the cavalry when at a distance of five or six rods, and if there is any thing that shows hostile intentions, then to make one dismount and give the countersign. At one time, after dark, a cavalry man's horse had got away, and came galloping towards Uncle Dan. His spirits rise—rise as the clattering hoofs come nearer, till within fifteen or twenty rods: "Halt!" he cries, three times in quick succession, and in a half second more the crack of his rifle would have brought us of the reserve to our feet, when his laughing comrades tell him the horse is without a rider.

As we came back to our comrades the next morning, I never saw them so desponding. The cold wind, the clouded skies, the open, filthy barracks, and the rebel armies—these are nothing to daunt: but Seward and Chase have resigned, (such is rumor); Burnside is defeated; a thousand times the worst of all, the North is distracted: "Will they support us?" "Will they support us?" ask many: "Woe on the heads of those infernal villains that stab our country in this dark moment," mutter others: "the South is united; foreign intervention is staring us in the face; a long winter is closing in upon us; Congress is a mob; some blaming this general; some, that general; and as if this was not enough, we have but about half rations." In the afternoon a cavalry man, who has gone a little beyond the picket line, is shot near an house by a bushwhacker. His comrades are furiously enraged: "To be shot in battle, to die on the field, for one's country," says one of the officers, "this is honorable—this is noble. We, who have lived for twenty months, as it were, in the saddle, who have endured the heats of summer, the colds of winter, with the blue heavens over us, the damp ground beneath us, with deadly foes prowling about us in our slumbers; we who have survived the wrecks of twenty battles,—we, I say, fear no danger. But to be murdered, butchered,—for, soldiers, look on our brother,"—(they have just brought him in, and he lies still bleeding on a board); "these villains have shot him through the heart; and his face, once so full of martial beauty, and his manly form, all mangled by a murderer's dagger, not a soldier's, by one that's loyal through the day, but traitor through the night. Men, we shan't endure this longer. That house shall no longer stand a rendezvous, where those who are loyal to our faces, disloyal to our backs, may congregate at night, and plot against our lives. Go, burn it to the ground, and if you set your eyes upon that murderer, never let it be said that 'that bushwhacker has killed another man.'" No sooner had he ended, than fifteen horsemen put spurs to their steeds, armed with pistols, cutlass and carbine, and in a short time the house is in flames, but the traitor escaped. On the 23d the cavalry are reinforced, so only two companies go on picket. The quartermaster brings a plenty of rations to us. On the 24th we are relieved by the fourteenth regiment, who arrive at our camp the middle of the afternoon.

DEC. 25.—Christmas. In all the brigade there is no drilling. The chaplains preach to the various regiments. Then many visit the Chantilly battle field. A citizen points out the spot where the brave Kearney fell: where the lines swayed to and fro. Here, side by side, are the graves of friend and foe. The enemy held the field. Their dead are buried very decently; but shocking to say, only a few sods were thrown over ours, and frequently, feet, hands and skulls are sticking out, flesh still on. But we found men from the twelfth regiment covering these heroes that fought so bravely. We lose another of our soldiers. Oscar Reed dies suddenly of typhoid fever.

DEC. 26.—Battalion and brigade drill; nothing new in camp—not even rumors. The weather is again quite warm; plenty of rations, and the boys cheerful.

Dec. 27.—"Is it battalion or brigade drill? Shall we go on a march, or be allowed to wash our clothes?" 'Tis noon; no orders have come; clean up for inspection. In two hours more all are scattered, a part getting wood; a part washing clothes, and themselves; others scouring guns. Now the long roll is beat. "Siegel is fighting at Dumfries." See the running, the scampering for arms. Two hours more; "no marching to-day," comes the order from the General.

Dec. 28.—Sunday. The usual inspection and divine services pass off: the soldiers write to their friends; stand out in the sun-light, laughing, talking, yet all quiet. Short are the hours, and quickly flies the day, hardly dreaming that we are soldiers. But just at dark one of the General's aids rides up to the Colonel's tent, on a gallop, as usual. In a moment the bugler sounds the officers' call. "Have your men ready to march at a moment's notice," is the order. Most expect to go; for we have heard of numerous fights for the past few days; of alternate victories and defeats: of marches, counter-marches and movements front, rear and flank, till we know not whether friends or enemies surround us. We are soon formed in line, and are off, expecting to have a little skirmish with rebel cavalry, after marching five or six miles. But when a little east of the village, we are placed in some rifle-pits dug by the rebels themselves, in the early part of the war, to oppose our advance. Two companies of the twelfth are sent forward that we may not be surprised. Report has swelled the number of Stuart's cavalry that have broken through our lines south of us, to four thousand ; as near as I could learn, about twice what they were. Two hours have passed ; some have unrolled their blankets, and are half asleep. Now a volley from the front. All spring to their places instantly, expecting the enemy. Cannon are planted to sweep the road. These are discharged a few times at the rebels, a mile and a half away, prowling around a house which they have set on fire. We then start for another road on double quick, glad to move ; for our hands and feet are getting numb with cold. Two hours here ; the companies are scattered about watching. "Who comes there ?" loudly cries the foremost of twenty horsemen. "Who comes there yourself?" replies the Colonel, each thinking the other an enemy. "I'm a Union picket and patrol between this and Centreville. Advance, and give the countersign." "Advance yourself, and give the countersign; I'm a colonel in the Union army, and here's my men about me." Soon they are satisfied with each other. The horses and men are hidden from us, before the clatter of their hoofs on the frozen ground ceases to reach us. A little after midnight we go back to the rifle-pits and remain till morning. We had but few cavalry near the village, so the enemy easily bent their course around us, with but little injury to themselves, and none to us. Before the sun has risen, little fires are started along the line, and around them soldiers cooking coffee and eating bread, and butter sent from home, or bought of the sutler for forty cents a pound. At eight o'clock the regiments return to their several camps and doze away the rest of the day.

DEC. 30.—Nothing but drills and guarding.

DEC. 31.—All are mustered. The boys do their best, at washing themselves and clothes, cutting hair and scouring guns, to show off as well as they can. The brigade head-quarters are established at the village, and for the past few days the regiments have taken turns in sending a hundred men to guard them. No little sensation has been produced by the arrest of several officers and privates, for not dressing, and washing, and stepping, and saluting, and other smaller things, just according to stern military rules. So before leaving our parade ground we go through a mimic guard-mount, under the eye of a field officer. We make a number of mistakes here. These are pointed out. And as is often the case, when, one not thoroughly versed in what he is doing, attempts at being over nice, comes short of his common work, so we under the eye of the General. Yet none are arrested; but some are sworn at, and one of the lieutenants laughed at for making a sort of an awkward start instead of a graceful salute as he passes the officer of the day. Two regiments of cavalry camped near the village. Some of these about midninght make havoc with the sutler's shops, helping themselves to the tobacco, beer, cider and apples, before the guards could reach them, declaring that they were "on a bust the last day of the year."

CHAPTER VIII.

JAN. 1, 1863.—It is a bright, sunny day—no clouds, no snow, or frost; the air pure and invigorating; the little birds seemed to have been thawed out, and skip about lively; the ground dry enough for good walking; in a word, everything in nature inclines one to enjoy the first day of the year. And so we do. A plenty of rations and no drilling; at our leisure we stroll and chat, and shake our sides with laughter at some good story; and Jack, Richard and Gibo, delight us with the fiddle, and now with songs of love and war; and a thousand youths in the whole brigade, with smiling faces,

> "Just at the age 'twixt boy and youth,
> When thought is speech, and speech is truth,"

I've heard saluting: "I wish you a happy new year;" and "I wish you a happy new year, too," as heartily as child ever did father and mother the first morning of the new-born year. O! may every day be lovely as this, boys, and no cloud come over your sun of joy.

JAN. 2.—Battalion and brigade drill. According to the regulations, every soldier, unless excused by the surgeon in the morning, (the captains can detail a few to do some little things, such as assisting the cooks, getting wood or water,) must attend the drills and parades during the day. Since here, quite a number have grown somewhat negligent. These are not out in the forenoon. The Colonel says nothing; but orders the regiment out in the afternoon in time for the sergeant to call the roll before starting for the brigade drill. Those who are not present, and not excused, are put under arrest and sent to the guard-house. As soon as we return, a court-martial is instituted to try them,—no, to frighten them. The next day they go through with a form of *trial*. They are charged with violating the forty-fourth article of war; and to this they plead guilty. But many are the reasons for it. Some were washing, and some cutting wood to stockade their tents, ignorant of the drill, they say, until the drums beat, and then they had not time to prepare for it; others say that they were unable to go, but could not get excused, and so took it upon themselves to remain in their tents. But it is all dropped; the Colonel advising the boys not to be caught committing a similar offence again.

JAN. 3.—All expected to start the next morning, when we encamped here on the night of 12th December. But we have remained day after day, thinking each day that we should go the next; or be ordered to "fall in" any hour of the same day, or night, to march. The nights are growing colder: so two days are given us, Saturday and Monday, to put small stockades under our tents, and make them as warm as we can. We lay out not as much labor on them as if we had not made so many and sudden moves; but some of the regiments have expended not a little time on theirs. Chestnut trees are slashed down, cut off the right length and split into slabs. A kind of a box, the bigness of the tent, three or four feet high, is formed out of these, the ends fitted together, the crevices, as usual, filled with mud.

The tents are placed on these, and are much warmer than before.

JAN. 6.—Dull, rainy; no drilling. Hardly a soldier is seen in the camp, except the guards pacing the beats. The President's proclamation causes a little discussion. Many are glad that it is issued, thinking it wise and just; wise, that by as much as you reduce the number of slaves laboring at home, so much you reduce the number of our enemies in the field; just, that all men should be free. Some think it impolitic, howsoever just; that it will serve to distract the North; now and then, one pretends to regard it unconstitutional. The next four days are spent in drilling, and making the tents more comfortable. In each one now you see a fire-place, or little stove, and a bunk to sit on through the day, and sleep on at night. Crotched sticks are driven into the ground; poles put on them; then these are covered with browse, or straw, if one is so fortunate as to get it of some farmer near by, whom the war has not entirely ruined. Of late, "When shall we be paid off?" is a question more frequently asked than any other, as we have been mustered twice without any pay.

A half dozen days have been fixed upon, by this one and that one. But these come and go, but not the paymaster. A sergeant comes into my tent. He has no sooner taken a seat on the little wood pile than two eager soldiers interrogate, "When shall we be paid off, sergeant?" "Paid off? I've been asked that question twenty times to-day; and the Lord only knows, I don't, as ever." "I'm a little blue to-day, boys, and the bump of hope was never as big in my cranium as in some others. If the government goes down, I wouldn't give 'a red' for a cart load of green-backs." "Goes down! what do you mean?" "I mean, if the South gets her independence, this flood of paper money won't be worth the rags that it's written on. The battles control gold, and it goes up and down as they turn for or against us, as a thermometer just as it is hot or cold. Like the snakes in the Eastern tale, that never showed themselves in the pure light of day but crawled forth at night from their slimy caves to hiss and bite, so a class is rising in the North, in this dark hour, to strike down our government. To tell it as it is, boys, I fear them more than the 'rebs.' But

I always seize on some sunshiny day, and when I am in tip-top spirits, to write home, and so they think I'm the best feeling soldier in all Dixie. In fact, I've written them that I was going to enlist again, so pleased was I with the service, partly to see what they would say, and more that they might not think me at all discouraged."

JAN. 11.—Sabbath—rainy; nothing but inspection in the morning, and guard-mount. Every soldier expects the guard-mount each day as much as his meals. The new guards and their arms are here inspected by a lieutenant, divided into three reliefs,—(each usually on duty two hours,)—then one is sent to take the places of the old guards around camp.

JAN. 12.—Company and brigade drills; and mud in abundance.

JAN. 13.—A dry place; one free from the wind, in cold weather; and near wood and water. These at least are necessary for a good camp ground. When we first came here this location answered to these. But now the ground is soaked with water, and it does not run off freely; some are sick; and a few have died very suddenly. The surgeons pronounce the place unhealthy, and think that the camp had better be moved. So we work during the day, policing the ground to the right of us. The next morning at two o'clock we are aroused by the "long roll." All are up in a few minutes. The first man I met after I was out of my tent, began: "What in hell is to pay now? Some men are scared at their own shadows. There a'int 'a reb' within a thousand miles of here." We don't leave the company streets, and in a half hour are told that we can lie down again. A bushwhacker had fired at a cavalry patrol not far from camp.

JAN. 14.—There are doubts whether the new ground, cleared yesterday, is more healthy than that we now occupy. Some of the field officers ride around to seek a better site; we stroll at our leisure. Rumor says that we are going to be transferred from the Department at Washington, and going to North Carolina. A part would like to go; others, not; the most think it only a rumor, and not worth an observation.

JAN. 15.—As soon as breakfast is over, all the companies, led by the major, with spades and axes, start to clear another place for the camp. We have a plenty of rations; it is a warm day, and most are in excellent spirits. But the boys look at each other, laughing, and say: "This is putting down rebellion in earnest." We are soon on the ground,—a dry side hill,—near a grove of Norway pines, a hundred rods to the left of the twelfth regiment. It is covered with logs, brush, and tree-tops. But the work goes bravely on. The streets are marked out for each company: and each clears its own. At noon we go back for dinner, carrying our axes and spades; for one, if he happens to be in want, does not scruple from other regiments, or any other company but his own, to steal such things, reasoning in this way: "These tools belong to Uncle Sam; I am working for the old fellow; this axe is better than mine, and I can do more work with it; so much clear gain!" This argument has morality enough in it to still the consciences of most soldiers if they have chopped long with a dull axe, and have a chance to get their hands on a sharper one; and so much logic, that no one pretends to refute it, only, if he has lost one, by improving the first opportunity that he has to steal another. In the afternoon we nearly finished policing the ground.

JAN. 16.—Raining till noon. The rest of the day we are stockading. Each squad builds its own. Two cut down the trees; two carry them on their shoulders to the spot; and the others fit them together.

JAN. 17.—A cold and windy day; but some work on the stockades; the rest remain in camp. I called into a soldier's tent; here I found four or five talking about the draft that was to take place the August before, as it is rumored that more men are to be drafted soon. Each has a story to tell of this or that one, who is suddenly taken sick, or runs to Canada, when the enrolling officer comes around. This one's eye-sight is very poor; that one, a little deaf; this one has humors through the cold weather; that one, the rheumatism; the fifth one is more than forty-five; but, alas! poor fellow, the family record in his father's old Bible says he is only forty-two. "Three groans," says the soldier, "for him, and all that utter a syllable against the government of the United States, or against the boys who march under the stripes and stars. Three groans now." Whereupon they exercise their lungs, as though they intended to be heard in the farthest north.

JAN. 18.—Last night water froze two inches in the little streams near camp. The day is quite cold; but we have inspection and divine service.

JAN. 19.—We start off and work about two hours on the new quarters, (the cold compels us to move briskly,) when orders come from some higher source, and we soon shoulder our spades, return, and exchange them for the rifles, and go to drilling. The old brick tavern in the village is used for the brigade hospital, where are brought, from the regimental hospitals, those who are the most dangerously sick. The bodies of nearly all who have died in our brigade have been enbalmed and sent home, at the expense of the companies to which they belonged. In the afternoon there was a funeral. The soldier died last night at the village, and wished to be buried there, saying that his wife could not endure the sight of his dead body.

The chaplain, musicians, his company, and such as choose to from the regiment, follow him to the grave. He is placed, before leaving the hospital, in a government coffin, made of boards painted black,—with the clothes on that he wore when alive. He is now laid in the ground four feet deep; twelve of his comrades fire their farewell shots; the chaplain speaks consoling words, offers a prayer to God and pronounces a benediction; and we turn away, not as when we came, with a slow and measured tread,—the drummers beating the dead-march,—but with quicker steps, a livelier air,—Yankee Doodle.

As we reach camp it is noised about that we are going on a march to-morrow.

CHAPTER IX.

JAN. 20.—"Is it forward or backward? to Bull Run or Alexandria? Are we really going, or is it another rumor?" Last night, with these queries in their minds, the soldiers closed their eyes; and this morning at five, they are pulled open by the beat of the drum. Soon the camps are all lighted; the rolls called; things packed; the mule teams loaded; and we are marching a little after day-light. We have gone but a few rods, when one comes from the brigade hospital to our company: "John Canady is dead," he says: "died at midnight." "John Canady is dead," passes down the line from mouth to mouth. The next day a soldier goes back to see that his body is sent to his friends. None have any regrets at turning their back on this place; for the brigade has four dead men now in the hospital, and a hundred and fifty sick,—some with typhoid fever, but most with the measles. We have reached our destination the middle of the afternoon—a high bluff near the Occoquan river, (twelve miles march,) with aching backs and weary legs. A soldier's burden (nearly fifty pounds) is much heavier this season of the year than in the summer. Now he clings to his blankets, shirts, &c., as to his life; then he threw them away on long marches to save it. As soon as it is known that we are to halt here through the night, all are working in great haste. The trees (for we are in a pine forest) fall as if the men were clearing the land. The tents are close behind us; and pitched before dark. We have no stoves; no brick with which we can make fireplaces; and the ground is frozen.

At night I go over the camp. Each company has eight or ten fires between its two rows of tents. Here is a small one, where are four or five soldiers chatting; there is one that roars, and lights up the woods for rods, its cone-like flames darting up ten feet and spreading as they curl among the spitting pine twigs and leaves. There is no war-whoop sounding out on the night air; no wild dance, or painted faces; but the scene really brings to mind the Indian stories of one's childhood. But no,—soon there are signs of civilization, and of a fiercer war than of bows and arrows. A battery of brazen cannon follows us, and is planted to defend the fords of the river; and the telegraph, with its lightning tongue to herald the least move of the enemy at any other point, is strung through the forest: and each man, though armed with rifle, has a copy of the New Testament. The brigade is now scattered; two regiments are here; the other three at Fairfax Station,—eight miles in the rear.

JAN. 21.—It rains fast all day. Some of the soldiers suffered considerably from lying on the ground last night. There were not axes enough so that all could make themselves bunks. Two teams reach us, lightly loaded with hard tack,—it is so muddy.

JAN. 22.—A captain, two lieutenants and one hundred men are detailed to turn the road where it is muddiest; and near evening the teams arrive with most of the baggage and some rations. Illy fares the mules and horses that have fallen into the hands of the government. Many fine animals—often by improper use—are spoiled in a short time; and now their bodies and skeletons line the fields and roads, where the armies have moved. Such of the sick as are able to walk, come up with us; for walking, as one can turn his course around the worst places, is much easier than riding over these roads. We also get our mail. No drilling; no skirmishing;—but rumors, thick as flies before a storm, and of about the same importance,—doing no injury, but still tormenting; these by little bites; those by setting curiosity on tiptoe,—now spreading events before you as you would like to have them, and on a sudden topsy-turvy every thing is turned. "The whole army is in motion," they say. "Burnside has crossed the river and captured eight thousand prisoners." One company pitches its tents on the scraggy side of the bluff in some bushes, near to and in sight of Wolf Run Shoals,—the name of one of the fords that we are to guard.

JAN. 23, 24.—The army of the Potomac is still on the Rappahannock. A few days ago they made a move, but were wholly impeded by the mud. Indeed, it is almost impossible to get provisions to us, only eight miles from the Station. The six mule teams flounder through, covered with mud from hoof to ear,—with loads hardly heavier than the same number of men could carry. We are thirty-five miles in the rear of the main army. Here is a long line of pickets on the outmost edge of the Department of Washington, guarding each pass from the Bull Run mountains to the Potomac. At many points the pickets are posted within sight of each other, but nearer the Potomac, where the water is deeper, only the fords are guarded: and these sometimes by infantry, and sometimes by cavalry. Yesterday ten paroled prisoners, that belonged to Gen. Slocum's corps, came into our camp. They had been captured a few days ago a little in the rear of the main body, whilst going through to Fredericksburg.

Our tents are now stockaded: in each is a bunk, and a good fireplace made of mud and stones. Many carry in their arms, or on the shoulder, long stones for mantel-pieces, a half mile. Twenty-five men, a sergeant and lieutenant, guard Sally Davis's ford, about a mile down the river.

JAN. 25.—At half past eight the drum beats, and soon twenty-five men are assembled before the Colonel's tent as pickets, equipments on, armed with rifle, blankets rolled and thrown over the shoulders. As soon as the guns are loaded, we start, led by the lieutenant, down the steep bluff, up and down another, and then along the muddy banks of the river, till we come to the old pickets, in a clump of pines, near the ford. The arms are stacked ; one is posted on the beat close to the river ; wood chopped for the fires ; a sort of burrows of pine limbs constructed, sometimes large enough for only two, and then simicircular around a fire, where a dozen crawl in at night. It is a warm spring-like day, and the boys enjoy it much, chatting, writing letters, reading newspapers, preparing dinner and supper. As eight or ten stand around a fire boiling coffee, "It is a beautiful Sabbath," says one, who has just come in from filling his canteen at a gurgling stream running down between two hills, and who doubtless had been led to meditate, as he, walking alone, saw the golden sun so gloriously setting in the west. "Is it Sunday?" reply three or four at the same time ; "is it Sunday ? I can hardly keep the days of the week, time flies so fast." With us were five

Michigan cavalry. All but one take no note of time. He would be delighted to see the sun doubling her speed, and the months huddled into days; they can hardly tell whether it is January or March, and certainly don't care. Says he: "Eighteen months ago I enlisted; left the best wife in the world, and haven't seen her since: had a good farm, and easily got a good living; came with no other ambition than to serve and save my country. Many is the time that I have sat all night on my horse, and slept by turns as he was going, or lain with the bridle about my arm." Another boasts that he had descended from revolutionary sires; that he had a boy in the Western army, and "one that will fight, too;" that he himself had been in twenty charges, and never received a wound; but that many a rebel had been slashed with his old sabre; that he would pass the rest of his life in war, before he would see the Federal Government go down; that this was the greatest war that ever raged on the face of the earth, and that the men who took part in it would be dearer to our descendants for transmitting liberty to them, than those that fought under Cromwell or Washington. The next morning we are relieved and arrive in camp about ten o'clock. Besides the pickets and guards, two hundred men are detailed in the rifle pits, to prevent the enemy crossing the ford near the camp. There are ditches, running zigzag, so deep as to protect the soldiers, with the dirt thrown towards the place from which the attacking party is supposed to come.

JAN. 27.—The same number of pickets, guards and men to work on the rifle-pits are detailed to-day as yesterday. But before noon it begins to rain, and the men on fatigue are called in. There are various rumors flying through camp. "Burnside has thrown up his commission. His soldiers have thrown down their arms, declaring that they would not fight any longer."

JAN. 28.—Stormy; sleet and snow falling all day; but the pickets and guards tie the haversacks close to their necks, and rubbers over the shoulders, and start to relieve those who have been on duty for twenty-four hours, knowing that they, too, will be relieved the same hour to-morrow morning. Slowly, slowly, wear the hours away, as the boys sit in the leaky bough-houses; snow and rain now and then splashing through the pine shelters; and nothing heard all day—all night—save the roar of the muddy waters of the river rushing madly by them. Before morning the snow is a foot deep in the fields; but this mud—mud—in the roads.

JAN. 29.—The boys have waited patiently since they have been mustered, for their pay. Some are really in need of it; fathers, whose families depend mostly on their wages. Nearly all are out of money; and a soldier actually needs a little, though fed by the government. If he is unwell, and we happen to be living on hard tack, he wants a piece of soft bread, piece of cheese, or butter, which he can get of the sutler by paying a high price. Some, however, are better off without a cent. More than one soldier have we seen unfit for duty; and the surgeons say, "He buys too much stuff of the sutler. He eats too many luxuries." The paymaster arrives about dark, and we receive two months' pay in green-backs. During the next four days it rains and snows alternately. We are almost blocked in with mud. A six mule team, now up, now down, wading through, comes in with two barrels of pork. Each day a hundred and fifty are detailed to build corduroy roads. These are divided into squads, strung along, and then work busily till they meet. We cover the old road with trees from four to ten inches in diameter, mostly pine; but if there are any chestnuts near by, we take these, being soft to cut and fissile. Some cut them down; some carry them on their shoulders, and others place them side by side. By the 5th of February, two-thirds of the eight miles from the Station to camp, is corduroy road. About this time I called at a citizen's house to get a meal of victuals. The old man was killing his hogs, and scalded them by putting hot stones into the tub of water. His house stands in the centre of a cleared spot, all surrounded by pine forests which have been encroaching on him for years. A Union soldier, one unable to do much duty, guards his property. As I approach and make known my errand, I soon observe that the owner is not in the best of humor for some reason, when he turns up his red face and stares at me with his blood-shot eyes: "Buy," he mutters, "soldiers buy? They've stole all I've got that they could carry away—them devils that followed Dan Sickles—my potatoes, my turkies, and most all my cattle. I never had any niggers; don't want them; but if soldiers should come into your country and steal your goods, wouldn't you fight? By the G—ds, wouldn't you fight? I still love the old Union; but I reckon it will be a long time before things are settled; and that proclamation will only make more difficulty. Oh, this terrible war! It will kill us all, I fear. We can hardly live here between the two armies. All the soldiers won't steal; but there are some thieves in the army as everywhere, and when they are going through here they take what they want, and I suppose the generals don't know it. You see this is a bad way of living; but, soldier, I'm a Union man, and if you want a meal, go in, and the women will get it." At which I go in; soon sit down to the table of hoe-cake, cold beef, cabbage and coffee. As the tract of land all around here is now held by Northern, now by Southern soldiers, then by neither, but the scene of almost single combat, where cavalry patrols on both sides scour, where you can trace many and long lines of pickets by the ashes of their posts, where guerrillas lurk, where great armies have met and fought most furiously, and the field sometimes held by one side and sometimes by the other,—so loyalty and disloyalty, by turns, hold sway over the minds of most citizens, near where we have camped.

FEB. 6.—Since here we have not got our mail daily. This the boys don't like, and blame the postmaster for it. Whisky rations (a rare thing with us) were dealt out to the soldiers last night. The Army regulations say: "One gill of whisky is allowed daily, in case of excessive fatigue and exposure." From this time till the middle of March, our "fatigue and exposure" were regarded so "excessive" as that when the guards and pickets came in, the coldest and stormiest mornings, the lieutenant takes them to the commissary, who gives each a small drink. But last night it was otherwise. The most drank it; some saved it for future occasions, when possibly they might be sick; a few sold it to those too fond of it. So occasionally one gets so much that he is noisy, and somewhat irregular in his actions. This morning one is drunk, and in for fighting. He speaks contemptuously to his lieutenant; strikes the corporal of the guard; pays no attention to the officer of the day; it takes four or five to manage him and get him in the guard-house, and he bites one of them quite badly. But he is not abused. He strikes them; but they do not return it, only hold him as well as they can. As soon as his hands are tied behind him, he gives up in despair, and the poor fellow cries like a child. The guard-house is a wall tent, and no fire in it; and being quite cold, when he comes to himself, so as to misuse no one, he is let out, and nothing more was done with him. To-day we draw soft bread, the first since we came here. But we get more fresh meat, as beeves can be driven and butchered here easier than pork or beef drawn through the mud. And our friends at home are ever mindful of us. Hundreds of boxes are sent to the brigade. Almost every day a load comes to our regiment, filled with butter, cheese, dried berries, and such as the soldiers need.

Feb. 7.—Save those detailed last night as guards and pickets, the rest remain quietly in camp: or some perchance stroll over the rough country around us. My friend, Sergeant Boyce, invited me and a few others to take supper with him, as he had lately received some things from home. He, as the others, had stockaded; that is, had built a sort of a pen with smallish logs, six or seven feet square, four high, filled the cracks with mud, and fastened his tent to this. Within is a floor made of slabs split out with the axe; in the corner, a small fireplace, (an aperture having been made through the side of the stockade, and on the outside a stack of stones for the chimney); on one side is a bunk, where three sleep, covered with blankets, and constructed of round poles; on it is a hard tack box,—a fine writing desk. Around the rough walls hang guns, bayonets, equipments, canteens and haversacks. He had fixed up a table for the occasion, running across one side of his castle, and blocking up the door, so that he has to remove a part of it for us to enter. We came a little early, and soon the sergeant

> "Turns, on hospitable thought intent;
> What choice to choose for delicacy best,
> What order, so contriven as not to mix
> Tastes not well joined, inelegant, but bring
> Taste after taste upheld with kindliest change—
> ——————— and on the board
> Heaps with unsparing hand."

plum preserves, mince pies, pudding filled with raisins, honey, and much more. Though the camp has been so quiet for several days, at eleven o'clock at night the long roll is beat and the soldiers spring for their arms.

CHAPTER X.

The picket line of the twelfth and thirteenth regiments has been extended up the river about five miles. Some of the fords are two miles apart; others in sight of each other. At some of the principal ones several cavalry are also posted, to report quickly to the headquarters, in case of a sudden attack, whilst the infantry are to prevent any crossing, if possible, but if not, then to retreat towards camp, firing. A little affair occurred on the night of the seventh, that caused some laughter among the boys. A cavalry man is standing on his beat, when he imagines (so say his comrades, and that he had given false alarms before, which is really a grave offence,) that he sees a rebel. Now he fires his pistol four times, and thinks his enemy returning the shots. The horse is scared, turns, and gallops towards the reserve, throwing off the more frightened rider. Instantly the pickets are out, for they lie down with equipments on, and the guns by their sides, running for the rifle pits. As they meet him, no cap on: "What's the matter? Are you shot?" quickly asks Capt. Blake. "No, no—theyv'e shot my horse under me. For God's sake don't let 'em across." By this time all are convinced that the coward is more alarmed than hurt; but the posts above and below have heard the reports, and pass the signal up and down the winding river, by discharging their rifles. Soon all is quiet; the soldiers in their bough-houses, save those on the beats possibly peering more sharply through the darkness.

For the next four days there is hardly a ripple in camp life, (then only small jogs). Indeed a soldier's life may be likened to a stream, to-day, calm and placid as the blue heavens; to-morrow, swollen beyond its banks, all the vale a surging sea, sweeping on with terrible fury, and after many fair and sunny days it returns to its old channel. You see a thousand faces together, none looking just alike, yet so near, it might even tax the painter's genius to point out each difference. So are many quiet days in camp, one very *like* the other.

Feb. 12.—A hundred men are sent across the river, with spades and picks, to demolish a rebel fort, that covers the shoals, situated on a higher point than any on this side. To-day our line has been extended farther west; and just before evening more are called for as pickets. Hurriedly they start off, but do not reach their post till it is so dark that they can hardly see any thing. For two miles they pick their way through the forests and thick underwood that stand on the rough bluffs of Bull Run.

Feb. 13.—Now every street in camp is corduroy, that is, between the rows of tents, and a long one running in front of the officer's quarters, up by the hospital, commissary's and sutler's. To the 26th, no change; nothing but picketing, dress parade, guarding, target shooting, getting rations, cooking, and the thousand and one little things for amusement. There is a little snow on the ground; but the middle of the day is warm, and frequently one-half the regiment is arrayed against the other, throwing snow balls, as they were wont in their school-boy days; and, when one side gives away, then comes the rush, the boisterous laughter, and the shout of victory, quite as loud as if it were no mimic fray. Many while away the evening hours before tattoo, writing letters, reading newspapers and chatting: some playing cards or checkers, now for fun, and now betting the apples or raisins, and when the game is over, the loser starts for the sutler, and soon returns with them; some whittling rings and pipes out of the laurel root, beautifully engraving on them the American eagle, the stripes and stars, and patriotic inscriptions like this: "Union and liberty, now and forever."

The health of the brigade is fine. We get soft bread three days out of five, and fresh beef in the same proportion; a daily mail: wood and water easily; and as the nights grow shorter and warmer, all, unless it happens to storm, had as lief go on picket as remain in camp. The 26th and 27th are warm and pleasant days, like those the last of March in New England. You meet one, and the first remark, after saluting, is, "'t is a beautiful day"; "a lovely spring-like morning;" "spring is coming," and such like expressions.

No small change is observable in the papers that came about two months ago, and those that have arrived lately. The editorials of the former were full of despondency; of the latter, hope and courage. We give a few extracts:

"As when in a great storm, the elements furiously warring, and the angry bolts seem to have wasted their strength, and roll muttering off, as if to gather new force, there is a sort of a pause, a lull, though deep, black clouds hang over head and all around, so now in our national affairs, after the three great and terrific battles that have just closed, 1862 went out in blood. The last ten days were passed in gigantic battles. Three times we struck at the enemy,—at Fredericksburgh, Murfresboro' and Vicksburgh,—and twice the blows were parried, and heavier ones dealt on ourselves; and this moment the nation is staggering. Or, the least that can be said, these defeats operate on the people as it does on one, when he has taxed all his powers, mental or physical, or both, toiling, day and night, month after month, cheered on by the hope of success, and then finally fails, utterly fails."

"It is of no use to conceal the truth. The fall campaigns have been most disastrous to us. After the battle of Antietam,—the rebels retreating, and our own recruits were pouring in so fast,—all were looking for the capture of Richmond. But for this, it is a defeat, a great slaughter, on the Rappahannock, a repulse at Vicksburgh, and a drawn battle at Murfreesboro'."

"Gloom, impenetrable gloom, hangs over the land."

"This revolution seems to be an exception to most others. No man has yet risen in the field, or the councils of the nation, equal to the crisis."

But gradually the people have risen above those defeats, and the papers speak in a different tone:

"If one were to judge to-day, by the appearance of nature only, by the cold winds, by the fields again white with snow, he would think it the middle of winter;

but if he walked out yesterday morning, and saw how the tender grass was shooting up fresh and green; how the buds of the trees were beginning to swell; how the solar rays did not fall so obliquely as last December; and how the newly returned birds were making the air vocal with their song, he would have exclaimed "Summer is at hand." So might one, in times of our defeats,—if he looked only at that defeat, as many do judge in this way,—say: "The rebellion will succeed"; but when we consider how much territory, how many cities and strong holds we have captured from the enemy, there can be no doubt as to the result of this war."

"The present Congress is showing itself equal to the tasks before it; and what is better, the people give unquestionable signs that they had rather sweat blood and gold much longer than see the unity of the Republic destroyed."

"There is a fly in some parts of Africa, that is wont to sting the natives on the leg. It leaves a little egg, and from this grows a snake, dark, poisonous, some two feet long. If it is extracted, and no part of it left, to poison the system, the afflicted man recovers. Like this has slavery grown up in America. At the formation of our government it was but a little egg in the giant leg of liberty. But from it has sprung the monstrous serpent of slavery. The enemies of our country—more unwise than the simple African—oppose extraction, and go in for amputation. Now this war will produce a complete extraction; the wound will finally heal; and we shall have a strong central government, around which will revolve these many states, as the planets around the sun; and the whole continent dedicated anew to Liberty and to God."

"This is but a continuation, on this continent, of the great struggle that has been going on in Europe for ages, between slavery and liberty. Who, after such examples as the German Puritans set, in opposing the Papal despot, can think of abandoning the sacred trust committed to us?"

"Who can estimate the importance of closing a war successfully, especially, if as here, it is between two civilizations? The effects of Alexander's campaigns, which took place more than two thousand years ago, are still visible in Asia. Whichever side finally triumphs in America, it is clear, that its civilization will inevitably spread over the rest of the continent. Since this is so, if we could afford to submit to the destruction of the Federal Government; to give up the Mississippi into the hands of a foreign power; to exchange the sea coast for a zigzag boundary line; and much more; certain it is that we never can, never shall suffer a slave oligarchy to dominate over the American continent."

If there is any thing more important than that American soldiers should be fed well, clothed well, and paid well, (as they are,) it is, that they should know to a certainty, as long as there is a single dollar or man that is able to bear arms, left in the North, that the war shall never be abandoned till every armed foe of the Republic is subdued. If any one wishes to make his friend uneasy in the army, he had better send him those papers which are continually finding fault with the administration, and with the conduct of the war in the field, and predicting defeat to our armies and ruin to our nation.

"They fly!" "They fly!" "Who fly?" "The French." "I die in peace," breathes the expiring Wolfe. Next to the Christian's hope, that which is most consoling to a soldier, if he must fall, is to know that his life is not to be given in vain. But I must close my writing now; for the adjutant has just hurried down the line of officers' tents; sticks his head in and says, "Be ready to march at a moment's notice;—two day's rations."

CHAPTER XI.

"Come, gentle Spring, ethereal mildness, come!"

A not much greater change is observable in nature than in the soldiers. Faces are brighter; steps quicker; many, who complained two months ago, praise now, and say, "A soldier's life is not very hard, after all." Spring, with its fresh breezes, is always welcome, though one dwells in a palace; how much more so to we soldiers, that live, as it were, in the open air. It is so warm that the boys bathe themselves in the little stream near camp. Yesterday a few rebel cavalry made a dash on our picket line to the west of us. As soon as it is known, it is telegraphed to Fairfax Court House, and thence to us. But they were soon beaten off, and we were not ordered to march.

MARCH 2.—Since we came here, there has been no drilling, on account of the snow and mud. To-day there was battalion drill. At night, after most are lain down, orders are sent through camp for all to be ready to march. There is not much of a stir. All place their guns and equipments where they can get them quickly in the dark. Soon the soldiers are asleep, and never knew why the orders came, only that there were rumors of the enemy near us.

March 3.—Battalion drill.

March 4.—The whole day is spent in cleaning the camp. The streets are swept, brush picked and burned, sinks filled up and new ones dug, cook stands and tents examined by the surgeon, and censured or praised, according to their neatness; in short, there was a general "clean up," just as the ladies, after the winter has passed away and spring returned, have their houses scrubbed and white-washed from cellar to garret.

March 9.—Nothing has occurred till this morning to break the monotony of camp life. Frequently we have heard of the raids of guerrillas, always above or below us, but never in front, on some part of the picket line; and so frequently have we been ordered to be ready to march at a moment's notice, that most care no more for such orders than when they come for us to fall in for dress parade, which we have at half past four or five in the afternoon of each day. Indeed, last night I heard a soldier talking to some others in this way: "Dr. Kane shows us in his Polar Expedition that one's appetite changes as he goes from a warmer to a colder climate, and that he really hankers after more fat; just so now and then you see one whose thirst for rebel blood increases or decreases, as he goes North or South, near or farther from the enemy; and some of those hypocrites at home, all out of harm's way, are perfectly ravenous." "Good! for that militia bill that's just passed Congress," breaks in another. "I know some ten or fifteen miserable copperheads, and some that don't belong to the snaky tribe, who preach war up to the handle, that might as well be here as you and I. But, boys, nothing would suit me better, although I might run, than to get my eyes on to a live rebel, to see what kind of *animal* (accenting the last syllable) he is; but I don't believe we ever shall."

The brigade is situated as it was when we first came to this place; two regiments here, three at Fairfax Station, and the headquarters at Fairfax Court House, a little more than four miles in the rear of the nearest of our regiments, and guarded by nearly a hundred men. But there usually were a body of cavalry camped near them. This morning it was telegraphed to Col. Blunt that the rebels had made a raid on the village last night; carried off Gen. Stoughton, his aids, guard, and some fifty horses. In a moment the news runs through the regiments. Some believe it; others do not. But it is soon known to be a fact that they had made a sudden dash and carried off the General, a few guards and a number of horses. The gang was led by Mosby, and came in to the west of our picket line. They enter the town slyly, not far from midnight, capturing the guards on their beats, one by one, not even disturbing the reserve. A few, easily overpowering the guard in front, go into the General's house and quickly rouse him from sleep, with no alternative left, but to dress, mount his horse, and ride rapidly as possible till out of the reach of pursuit. There were fifty of the rebels. All escaped with their booty, with no injury, as they got two hours the start of our cavalry. All day there is much talk about this little affair, how many prisoners, how many horses, how much propererty, and how much the start of us they had got. Col. Blunt assumes command of the brigade. We hear nothing more from the enemy till the 12th, when it is telegraphed that their cavalry were crossing the Rappahannock, in order that our pickets might keep a sharper look out.

MARCH 13.—You see the soldiers out as in January, gloves and overcoats on. carrying wood for fires in their tents:

> "As yet the trembling year is unconfirm'd,
> And winter oft at eve resumes the breeze,
> Chills the pale morn, and bids his driving sleets
> Deform the day delightless."

By this time we have cut out and burned the most of the timber on a number of acres near camp. One would hardly think that we pitched our tents in a thick forest. But such it was, on the top of a high bluff, sloping east and west, and running north and south down to the Occoquan. At night the enemy, emboldened by their first success, make another raid on Fairfax, of about the same number as before. But instead of catching a General, they lose seventeen horses and the same number of men, (such is rumor,) who are sent to Washton. The headquarters of the brigade are now at the Station.

MARCH 15.—In the afternoon the long roll is beaten; the regiment called into line; arms are stacked, and we are told to be ready to start at a moment's notice. A few guerillas came down the other side of the river and fired at some of our cavalry; but this was all, and the last that was seen of them. The pickets were strengthened during the night. The camp guards have been allowed, through the cold weather, to go to their tents as soon as relieved; but lately one relief has been kept at the guard-house all the time, as rebel cavalry are prowling about more nights. These are not large bodies, varying from ten to two hundred. Many of them are citizens, clad in the uniform of Union soldiers, who know every hill, valley, by-path and hiding place from the Potomac to the Rappahannock. Says one, and so some think, when chagrined by some of their midnight exploits, that neither hastens the war to a close or protracts it: "I would like the conduct of the war long enough to set the torch to every house in Dixie. Ought the heads of these vile traitors to be sheltered for one night even, here almost in sight of the tomb of Washington, who spring like tigers at the throat of the freest and best nation on the face of the earth?" But another replies: "Revenge dictates in this way; but 'revenge, at first, though sweet, ere long back on itself recoils.' One of the most disgraceful acts recorded in history, is, that the king of France once burned every house in a district in Germany, and thereby sent half a million of women and children homeless and beggars into the world. Now, since this war could not be avoided, we ought to thank Heaven that so good a man as Mr. Lincoln is at the head of affairs. We call him too lenient; the rebels, too severe,—a sure sign that he is about right. When we call to get a meal of victuals at any of the citizens', they treat us well, and do not ask a high price for what they sell us. Whether the *men* are loyal or disloyal, or neutral, it will not do to turn the women and children houseless into the country."

March 17.—Yesterday it stormed, so we start for the picket line this morning in four or five inches of snow; but about noon it begins to grow warmer, and before the next day the fields are bare. The river rises rapidly. Almost "palpable darkness" hugs the valley. Only two nights before, a cavalry post of five was captured three miles below us. This, and a few rumors, open the boys' ears. The sound of the rising stream, spreading over new lands, dashing against different stones and trees, changes of course every movement. As one's thoughts, when walking his beat, turn away to other scenes,—home and friends—and then return, the river is thundering in a strange jargon. Then the picket, ever present, ever watchful, stoops and strains his eyes to peer through the dark. "It may be a 'reb.'" is the first thought. One, just above me, taking deadly aim at a skulking bushwhacker, shoots his rifle at midnight; but shoots into the noisy, rushing waters. The report rolls up and down the wandering Occoquan, from post to post. The sleepy boys (not those watching now) lying around the fires on cedar or pine browse, covered, feet, head and body, with blankets, start up instantly, and in a low tone: "What's that?" "Is a gun fired?" "Hark! hark!"

says the picket on the beat: "only *one* yet." They, leaning on their elbows, listen awhile; and hearing no more reports of rifles, lie down again to their sleep, muttering: "Some fool was frightened." As we were going back the next morning to camp, the soldiers, for sport, ask Hucklebone many questions about the "reb" he had killed.

On the 22d five cavalry come galloping into our camp bareheaded, and before it is fairly light. Some guerrillas had attacked the post just before morning, and captured a portion of it.

MARCH 24.—Before daylight a few sick were started off for the hospitals in Washington, in the ambulances. Fifty are sent over the river, in pursuit of wagons covered with cloth, as some thought; but when they reach the spot, only white cows are to be seen. Crossing and recrossing was accomplished slowly, as they were paddled over in a newly made boat that leaked so that two men were needed to dip out the water. A few days ago ten privates and two sergeants were detailed to act as scouts. One of these, just before roll call, comes into camp, who has "got track of some rebs," he says. So in fifteen or twenty minutes, ninety men and officers—all volunteers—are starting down the river, guided by the Scout of the Occoquan, a romantic nickname that somebody had given the to tallest scout, and one whose fondness for roving was never surpassed by a wild Indian's. It is a warm night, but dark, and at times raining furiously.

March 25.—Early five companies are scouting over the country within four or five miles of camp. I, with others, go on picket. Just as we were starting, those who had gone out the night before came plodding in. I see one stick his head out at the door of his tent, smiling, as he looked at the long streaks of dirt on their healthy faces, where the rain had coursed freely down during the night, and say: "What did you get, boys?" "Git!" replies an old Irishman, half in anger, "don't ye see we git tired legs, hungry bellies and wet backs." The fourteenth regiment is now camped near us; the fifteenth and sixteenth are at Union Mills; the headquarters of the brigade are there also. We have a pleasant day on picket; a plenty to eat of soft bread, fresh beef, sugar and coffee. The air is filled with the song of birds by day, and the ceaseless peeping of frogs by night. It is thought that rebel cavalry are within the lines; and hence we have orders to be very watchful, and send all to camp, who are wandering about the post, whether soldiers or citizens.

April 1.—For several days the camp has been unusually quiet; no rumors; no raids on any part of the picket line kept up by our brigade. Everybody has enjoyed to-day; warm, sunshiny; and almost all have been April-fools.

> "Theirs was the glee of martial breast,
> And laughter theirs at little jest."

During the afternoon it is noised about that we are going on a march in the morning. Many think that this is only a jest.

CHAPTER XII.

April 2.—So acquisitive a being as a Yankee cannot remain two months in one place without collecting more materials than one man ought to carry on a march. The soldiers this morning, after selecting the choicest things, slung their knapsacks, crowded to the utmost. The warm sun is shining on the fresh, green earth; the trees are just leafing out; the little birds are singing their sweet matins; and one can scarce believe that war, mad, furious and desolating war, is in the land. But stop, only two nights ago they say that a picket post of twenty cavalry was captured, down the river eight or ten miles; and that we are going to defend the place. So it is. The loaded teams go around by the road; we, along the banks of the Occoquan, up and down ragged bluffs, so rough and steep that the regiment is scattered; one here, one there; the right wing only a quarter of a mile in advance, but still out of sight. At noon we halt; make coffee in our little cups, and eat dinner, of soft bread and fresh beef, which we have brought in the haversacks. Before two o'clock we and the teams have arrived at the place of encampment, near the main road running from Alexandria to Fredericksburgh, in a dense forest of pines. Immediately some are making stockades; but a stop is soon put to this, by the Colonel's saying that it was growing warm so fast there was no need of it. It is a hot day, and the sweat rolled down the soldiers' red cheeks like rain. Whisky rations are dealt out to all. Before night the tents are pitched, and most have constructed bunks of round poles to sleep on. At half past seven the long roll is beat, quick—quick,—as if the enemy were close upon us. The boys seize their arms, and almost instantly are in line. The reason of it was this: the woods seemed full of wild hogs, when we first came here. This is too tempting a lure for some. Though strict orders have often been read in the past against shooting guns near camp, the roar of the rifles comes thicker and thicker, mingled with shouts and boisterous laughter, as the bristly animal gives up the chase. But,

"Hark!" "The long roll! The long roll!" Now the legs of the excited hunters are flying through the dark forest, towards the blazing camp fires. But as they come in, they are taken and ordered to guard the camp during the night.

APRIL 3.—Early the Colonel rides around to discover the best site for a camp; and one company is sent on picket. By ten we are carrying our things towards the newly selected spot,—an open, level field, in sight of the Potomac; and yet pines are growing, now in thick clumps, and now more scatteringly, over the most of the plantation. The camp is laid out regularly. There are twenty rows of parallel tents; two for each company, with streets a rod wide. A little in the rear of these, and forming right angles with them, is the long line of tents belonging to the captains and lieutenants; next, those of the field officers; then you come to the hospital; and still on, among the trees, are hitched the horses and mules. Many lug, on their backs, poles for their bunks, from the last night's encampment. At the usual time we have dress parade, and also our mail.

APRIL 4.—One company a day does the picketing. There are three posts on the main roads near camp, and two fords and one ferry to be guarded. It is said that this line is to be defended by cavalry, and that we are going back near Washington. Time will show how this is. "We may stay here a week," says one; "and we may a month," replies another; "I've no care which it is, a week or a month," continues the next. "But wherever this brigade is, no rebel will turn his tracks that way, unless he has made up his mind to commit suicide, and takes that course to get rid of himself, suddenly and honorably." At half past eight my company is starting off to relieve the old pickets. A lieutenant, sergeant and ten privates are stationed at the ferry opposite Occoquan Village,—a place of some thrift before the war. A part of the inhabitants are loyal, a part disloyal; and both abandon their homes, and go back to them, as that army to which their sympathies belong recedes or advances; and still a third class call themselves neutral, a sort of amphibious animals, now in the slough of treason, and then out, whichever will profit them most. One is stationed on the beat at a time; and is relieved each hour. He gets the following instructions: "Keep a sharp watch up and down the river, and also in the rear of us; for it is reported that rebel cavalry are within our lines, and if they capture this post, they can cross and recross on the ferry as much as they choose." The rest of us are glad to turn into a very dirty shop, standing on the side of the bluff; for before noon it begins to storm, and continues till the next day, when we go back in a foot of snow. The soldiers at the two fords above us suffered far more than we, as they had nothing but bough-houses to shelter them. The boys are much delighted to exchange their salt pork for fresh herrings, which the citizens are just beginning to catch with their nets.

APRIL 15.—As we arrive in camp, we find that many have sought covering in the nearest houses and barns. The storm came upon us all unprepared. None have built fire-places, and but few have stoves. "This," says one, "is not so bad as a defeat; for it chills our bodies only and not our spirits." "The next disaster that befalls the Union armies," answers another, "I shall set down as a snow storm in April, which hides from us only for a day the sure signs of coming spring,—the wild flowers and the green scattering grass,—and soon the earth is fresher and greener than before. But if we've had a specimen of the 'sunny south', I'd as soon desert the girl I love best, and marry a wench, as, after the war, bid farewell to old New England, thinking to live on the barren plains and hills of Virginia." Those tents where there are fires, are crowded full. At night there is no roll-call, and early the boys lie down, covered with their blankets.

April 6, 7.—Both days are warm, and both are passed with us in making our tents more comfortable. On the night of the 7th, it is thought there is difficulty on the picket line, for some reason. So a lieutenant and twenty-five soldiers are sent down only a mile's distance, through the mud and dark; but the disturbance is only imaginary.

April 8.—Col. George J. Stannard is promoted Brigadier General, and assigned to the command of this brigade. Two regiments and the headquarters are at Union Mills; two at Wolf Run Shoals; and ours a mile north of Occoquan village, which is situated on the banks of a small bay of the same name; all keeping up about twenty miles of the front line in the Department of Washington. In the afternoon, battalion drill.

April 9, 10.—Drilling both days.

April 11.—The regiment is mustered. It is said that all are, to learn the exact number of fighting men. "What does this mean?" asks one, (for we commonly are mustered the last day of every other month). "It means," replies another soldier, "that we have fun with the 'rebs,' and 'right smart, too, I reckon,' (imitating the native Virginians;) fighting Joe is'nt the fellow to lie idle much longer. And when he strikes, he will give them a wound that won't stop bleeding in one day; and will send them running in a way they won't look back before they reach Richmond. So it wouldn't be very wonderful if the Second Brigade should be picketing on the Rappahannock instead of the Bull Run and Occoquan, next month. Or, some say that we shall be transferred into the army of the Potomac soon; and for my part I would like to see it, that we might prove to the old soldiers that they should call us 'Casey's lions' sooner than 'Casey's pets.'"

April 25.—In looking over my diary for the last fortnight I find nothing but "picketing," "guarding," "battalion drills" and "pleasant days." Though in the morning each company sweeps its street, in a short time, without the greatest care on the part of all, the vicinity of the camp becomes dirty. All the boys have been policing, that is, cleaning the camp and the adjacent lands.

April 26.—Review. In the morning, hair is cut, whiskers trimmed, boots made to shine a little brighter; in fine, the "finishing touch" is put on to everything, as our General is present, for the first time. The review passes off finely and agreeably to all.

April 27.—Battalion drill in the morning. At the close, the regiment is formed into a square; Gen. Stannard is introduced, and makes a short speech; the soldiers give him three loud and hearty cheers; then the officers are called forward, and introduced personally to him by Col. Randall,—the General shaking each by the hand warmly.

April 28.—Three or four from each company are usually permitted to visit Mount Vernon a day, which is about twelve miles northeast of our camp. Many have turned their faces that way to-day. But I will not give an account of our pilgrimage to this sacred shrine, since others have done it so often before; but suffice it to say that we had a most pleasant ride over the hilly, wood-covered country; and strange, though not unpleasing sensations, as we, as soldiers, looked in upon the sarcophagus holding the ashes of Washington; and also, most hospitable treatment at the loyal village of Accotink, where we put up during the night. This is the first time that I have slept in a bed since leaving home; but I have become so accustomed to my pine bunk, that my comrades affirm, after ten o'clock at night, the rebels could drag me off, without disturbing my slumbers.

April 29.—We receive four months' pay.

April 30.—Mustered.

May 1.—A holiday with us; warm and lovely as one can imagine. All, save the guards and pickets, take a stroll and come back to camp with a bunch of wild flowers or peach blows.

MAY 2.—Drilling; and rumors, that Hooker is moving; and we have heard cannonading the most of this afternoon.

PICKET POST, NEAR OCCOQUAN VILLAGE, VA.,
Sunday Morning, May 3, 1863.

MY DEAR FATHER AND MOTHER:—You will have heard of the great battle now going on near Fredericksburg, before this shall reach you. It is a still, Sabbath morning: not a cloud in the sky; and all nature clad in the freshness and beauty of spring. Since daylight we have heard the roar of cannon growing heavier and heavier, till now it almost shakes the solid rocks on which I am writing. Our brigade has not yet been ordered to move, and we may not be, though we could doubtless reach the scene of conflict before it will have ended.

SUNDAY EVENING.—We at this post have been busy all day ferrying sutlers across the river, who arrive from the army of the Potomac. They all bring one report: "Hooker is thrashing the rebels." They no sooner reach the opposite shore than some of our boys run quickly down and ask: "What's the news from the old army?" "Fighting; fighting all along the line; but we are laying them out good," and many such expressions. They say that a number of regiments have volunteered, whose time of service had expired, to fight during this battle. Our boys gave three cheers for them; and are ready to start any moment. All feel that Government has done what it can to make us comfortable. And now if this brigade is called upon to face danger, they will do it like heroes; mark that. But this picket line must be kept up, and we may not move at all.

MONDAY MORNING, MAY 4.—We heard cannonading until late in the evening. We are to be relieved from this post soon; have heard from camp, and the whole brigade is under marching orders, and expect to start in a few hours. You shall hear again as soon as affairs are more settled; but I must close now, as the postmaster will soon be on his way to Union Mills with the mail.

Your affectionate son.

CHAPTER XIII.

May 4, noon.—"The A tents, and every thing that we cannot easily carry on our backs, are to be loaded on to the wagons and sent at once to Alexandria," is the first thing we heard as we came in from the picket line. All in great haste are packing their overcoats, drawers, shirts (for hereafter each will have but two), and such as have two blankets, one of these, into boxes, to be carried to the rear. "This looks a little as though we were stripping for a fight," said a soldier, as he came into my tent, and found me in doubt whether to send one, or both, or neither of my blankets. "Should rather have none than carry two these hot days," he continued, "and we shall be off before night." Those unable to march and fight are carried to some general hospital.

May 5.—Early the heavy baggage is sent back. Our regiment still retains the A tents; the others have the shelter tents. We have heard some firing most of the day; are still under marching orders. As the P. M. comes in with papers, the soldiers fairly run to get them. One will read aloud in the open air, whilst fifteen or twenty are listening. In them are such headings as this: "Glorious News! Glorious news! Hooker is driving the enemy at all points!"

MAY 6.—Last night it rained, and is now much cooler. "Hooker has gained a great victory;" "thousands of prisoners are arriving at Washington;" "we shall be on the Rappahannock soon." These rumors are flying through camp. Still under marching orders; and still expecting, and ready and willing, each hour to go the next. The next two days are quite cold, dark and stormy.

MAY 9.—All are delighted to see the sun again, as they have parted with so much of their clothing. The most are convinced that the army of the Potomac has retreated to the north side of the river. Many are the opinions expressed as to how much injury each has received; some inclining one way, and some the other. About this time, Capt. Munson, of our regiment, is promoted Lieutenant Colonel, in place of A. C. Brown, resigned; and Capt. Boynton promoted Major, in place of L. D. Clark, resigned.

MAY 14—Pleasant days, and all quiet till this morning. At nine o'clock the orderly, who was carrying dispatches and the mail to headquarters, came galloping his horse into camp. "The 'rebs' have got the teams," he quickly cries; and "the 'rebs' have got the teams" quickly flies to every tent. There is a space of some two miles that is unfordable, between the two regiments, during the high waters of spring; and supposed to be so now, and hence not picketed. Here a little band of eight rebel cavalry cross, each armed with two pistols, and lie in ambush in thick trees. near where our teams almost daily go to the station,—out three miles from camp. As the three teams—twelve mules and four horses,—and with the drivers happened to be two sergeants, all unarmed—were just emerging from the dark forest, the enemy pounced upon them, cocking their pistols, and ejaculating: "Halt! halt! there, you d—d Yankees." Resistance is sure death, producing no good; for the rebels would have got the horses, which they were after. Soon all are mounted and steering for the river. Meanwhile we have heard of the affair, and start, now on quick, now double quick time, one company directly for the ford, and three others, down the road, and then on the tracks of the flying guerrillas. But alas! we come to the stream, tired, panting like blood-hounds, a little too late, just as the pursued have crossed.

MAY 15, 16.—Both days companies have been scouting over the river; and the result is, we have more horses than we had before our teams were captured. Our soldiers, who had been captured on the 14th, came in. They had been paroled, when a little south of the Bull Run battle field; but not according to the cartel. The last part of May is made up of pleasant days, one like the other; but not more so than the duties of one day are like those of the other. There is more sickness than usual in the brigade. My company lost two soldiers,—Cyren Thayer and Charles Billings.

MAY 29.—Since here, we have drawn all the soft bread that we can eat. But it is now getting so warm that it soon dries. So in each tent you see a cellar a foot and a half square, and as deep, and in it, moist bread and a canteen of cool water. Through April, cattle were driven up from Fairfax Station, from which are brought all of our rations, a distance of about eight miles, and butchered near camp, giving us what fresh beef we wanted. But during May, only a few have been slaughtered each week, owing to the hot weather. Many buy milk, and some eggs, of the citizens, and nearly all get what fresh fish they want. The most purchase them, or exchange some of their rations; but I have known of old fishermen, when on picket, sitting nearly all night on the rocks, hooking out eels and hornpouts. Since the ground has become dry, many are the amusements. After the drilling is over, towards evening, the wide, level space, in front of the camp, is crowded with soldiers. Many are playing ball. The most expert choose up, and one is to keep tally; now they strip off coats, and sweating and eager as to the result, push on the lively game. Some are pitching quoits, all boisterous, joyous as school boys at home. It is now dark, and one street is lighted, not with golden chandeliers, but candles stuck in bayonets, and these hanging in mimic shade trees. One is playing on the fiddle, another on the banjo, for the many to "chase the glowing hour with flying feet."

MAY 30.—On picket. The night is really splendid. The blue bay of Occoquan, many feet below us, gives back the shining moon and stars, the air not uncomfortably hot, and just wind enough to stir the luxuriant foliage of oaks near our post. Then there is the noise of the river to the right of us, (here it empties itself into the bay,) dashing against huge rocks; of the whippoorwill, singing its own name, by turns, all night, and often imitated by the soldiers; and of yelping curs, and now and then, loud baying, barking blood-hounds, disturbed in their kennels.

MAY 31.—May closes on Sunday. The review is just before evening, it being so hot.

JUNE 1.—There are many rumors of Lee's movements and of Mosby's raids. The latter had attacked and burned some of our cars, four miles south of Union Mills, but a few days ago, loaded with forage for the army of the Potomac. But Gen. Stahl's cavalry pursued, captured their artillery and a number of prisoners. We get daily papers from Washington, and many are the hopes and fears expressed after reading them, for Gen. Grant, in the rear of Vicksburg; and various are the opinions, now that he will get the stronghold, and now that he will finally be repulsed, as Sherman was the fall before. A soldier said to me, who carefully watches every move: "For a long while my friend was sick with the fever · and for awhile I anxiously watched over him, at one time seeming better and then worse; and when he went to the hospital, twice a day I used to call and see him, and as the disease was culminating, and I looked on his pale face and glassy, wandering eyes, I trembled and fairly held my breath, lest he should die any moment; but when I saw that he was gaining a little, my heart leaped with indescribable joy. So," said the noble soldier, "I've been watching over the brave boys in the rear of Vicksburgh, and can hardly wait for my daily paper to come in. O God, give them victory."

June 7.—The first days of June are hot, and camp life inactive. I have Paradise Lost with me, and have read, and re-read it. Not unpleasantly I have been passing a few days in perusing Tom Moore's works, which a soldier had borrowed of a citizen. As I closed Lalla Rookh, I could but think that a great many in our own country very much resemble old Fadladeen, the critic.. When he learns that Feramorez is no poor minstrel, but really none other than the King of Bucharia, and the bridegroom of the beautiful queen, his sour criticisms are changed at once into wonderful praises. Just so many of the opponents of the government are made friendly to it, as the tide of war turns. Indeed, we have seen some of these half traitors almost grow pale, and mute as a dumb stone, at the great successes of Grant around the key of the Mississippi, fearing to change their tone too suddenly.

We have just heard that Capt. Bostwick died on the 4th inst., at Washington. Capt. Whitney died a few days before at Alexandria. Their places are filled by the next ranking officers.

JUNE 14.—The twelfth regiment is now strung along the railroad running south, and guarding it. The boys of late have been feasting on strawberries and cherries, which they are allowed to stroll off and pick. It is Sunday, and unusually still and quiet. A little before noon an ambulance driver comes into camp. He is from the sixth army corps. What means this? The soldiers flock around him. "Where is Lee?" "Where is Hooker?" "Has he been beaten, or out-generalled?" He tells his story the best he knows. "Lee is off towards Warrenton,—he went around us; and Hooker is out that way, (pointing west). The sixth army corps is falling back to Alexandria." This is all; and this is enough to break the silence in the almost noiseless camp. The soldiers turn away, talking among themselves. "Another Bull Run battle, I reckon." "All right, we are good for 'em." Our regiment goes down and prepares the road a little; and soon the baggage wagons and artillery are crossing the river on pontoon bridges. The most of the soldiers turn off and cross at Wolf Run Shoals.

JUNE 15.—I happened to be one of the guard. The first thing that I heard this morning was from the ambulance driver that we spake of. Some one had stolen his saddle from under his head, when asleep last night, and he awoke me to help him find it; but to no use. Early the A tents are sent to the Station, and the small ones spread over the old sites to keep the sun off. All day artillery, teams, and now and then a regiment, have been going to the rear. "The rebels," they say, "are headed for Maryland, and you'll be fighting there to defend Washington, or at Bull Run, within a week." Gen. Hooker and staff passed about three o'clock.

JUNE 16.—We move our camp about a hundred rods, thinking it to be healthier. All carry their bunks to the new place. We have seen several officers from the army of the Potomac: "The rebels are headed for Maryland, and Hooker is after them. Shall have a third Bull Run battle." "They won't make much out of this strike." So all think.

EVENING.—Here, squads of ten or fifteen are gathered around some old soldier telling his tales of blood, or where he thinks the enemy are; there are many sitting on the ground, talking, laughing, singing, and some are smoking.

JUNE 17.—A hundred and fifty from our regiment have been to see their sons, brothers and more distant relatives in the First Brigade, which is now encamped near the Station.

Some, as soon as it was known where they were, started at midnight, and found them in a forest, asleep, and lying on the ground here and there "like sheep," as one expressed it. Brothers awoke brothers, and friends friends who left home near two years ago, and fought in every battle in which the army of the Potomac had been engaged; and though too dark to discern face or form, perhaps changed by toil or exposure or battle, but the voice is remembered, and they clasp each other with the affection of children.

JUNE 18.—On picket opposite the village. Quite a number have left the place, as they think rebel cavalry may dash in any hour; but we saw no signs of them. Two officers from Gen. Hooker's staff visit the line and report it "all right." I never saw the boys in better spirits. This post has been increased to twenty. There are two good story-tellers, and three or four that sing, who take turn in amusing the crowd, and no little fun and amusement is produced. During the next two days events are being shaped behind the curtain,—we spectators seeing and hearing just enough to set curiosity and anxiety chafing.

The pickets as they leave camp are reminded of their responsibility; that we are in the front line, guarding not only our own camps, but those of the army of the Potomac, which is mostly in the rear of us.

JUNE 21.—Sunday. We have heard firing the most of the day. Our teamsters at the Station saw the wounded brought in, and rebel prisoners going to Washington. They came from the west of us. There was a sharp cavalry fight near Snicker's Gap, leading into the Shenandoah Valley.

CAMP CARUSI, June 22, 1863.

MY DEAR SISTER,—Everybody moves but us. This picket line is still kept up. The boys were going to move long before, and fight the enemy; but not a rebel has been seen yet. The oft repeated question is, "Where is Lee?" Some say he is in the Shenandoah valley; others think that he is just south of the Bull Run battle-field. Gen. Hooker's army corps are within supporting distance of each other in the vicinity of Centreville and Fairfax Court House. It is reported that a few of the enemy have reached Pennsylvania, and that Harrisburg is in danger. We do not know what to think of these things, or how this great move will finally turn out. The soldiers are in good health and spirits. None expect a large force this way; but in case of a great battle near where the armies have met twice before, this brigade will doubtless take part in the bloody drama. The excitement is just enough for some, operating like wine on them.

Your affectionate brother.

JUNE 23.—We have our usual drill in the afternoon. At the close, arms are stacked; we go to our tents and eat a few hard tacks and drink a little coffee; read our letters just from home, and the drum beats for dress parade. Regimental orders are read, and Gen. Pleasanton's report of his victory over Stuart last Sunday. Then the Colonel steps forward and informs us that he had just received orders for his regiment to be ready to march at a moment's notice, with ten days' rations. I hear the soldiers whisper, "This looks a little like fighting." None can imagine the direction of our course. Such is Tuesday evening, with many rumors about the invasion of the North. At dark, teams are started for rations and return at daybreak. The troops around the Station have the same orders as we. Lee is thought to be in Maryland and intending an attack on Washington or Baltimore. If we move, this whole line, the Station, Centreville, Fairfax Court House, and all South of Alexandria, are to be abandoned, and we go North. The following short letter will show what the soldiers thought at night:

My Dear Sister:—These changing whirls have not yet caught us. Last night we received orders to be ready to march; but we have seen no signs of it during the day, and we may —— but I must change the tone of my letter at once, for an orderly has just come from headquarters to tell us that the whole brigade is to march in the morning. This monotonous drama is ended, and the next will close with the battle-field. May God shield the soldiers, and give them victory.

Your affectionate brother.

CHAPTER XIV.

JUNE 25.—As early as the 13th, General Milroy was attacked at Winchester, by the advance of Lee's army under Ewell, and retreated to Harper's Ferry. A force of rebel cavalry crosed the Upper Potomac on the 15th, causing no little consternation among the people of Maryland and Pennsylvania. The President sees the great danger, and calls for one hundred thousand more men from these two states, Ohio and Western Virginia, on the same day, to serve six months. On the 16th, a detachment of the enemy makes an attack on Harper's Ferry, but is repulsed by Gen. Tyler. During the night, ten thousand infantry are sent across the river at Williamsburg. As early as the 19th, the whole force under Ewell was on the north side of the Potomac; and by this time it is thought that a large part of Lee's army must be. Our brigade is transferred from the defences of Washington. and ordered to report to

Gen. Reynolds, commanding the first army corps, which is moving north, to oppose the invading foe. We leave camp a little before eight o'clock, with a slow step, we in the ranks not knowing where we were bound, whether west, or north to Alexandria. The regiment rested four times before arriving at Union Mills at one o'clock ; and there is far less falling out from the ranks than ever before. The day, though hot, is not excessively so ; but at every pure stream of water we pass, many run to fill their canteens. At the last named place the five regiments of the brigade come together ; and there is the most friendly feeling among all. Here we halt an hour and eat dinner. Before starting, it begins to rain, and continues at intervals the rest of the day. When it is growing dark we spread our little tents, which we have brought on our backs, using guns for stakes, a mile west of Centreville. Wet as every thing is, fires are started, and all have hot coffee and hard tack for supper. In a short time you hear but little noise in the camp ; the soldiers are asleep, wrapped in their blankets. Some have thrown theirs away, but crawl in by the side of others.

June 26.—Early every-body is preparing for the march. A part fill the canteens; a part kindle fires; and straightway coffee is boiled, and breakfast eaten. Now the tents are taken down, and with them the blankets rolled. Near by us we find bivouacked the old brigade, and the rest of the sixth corps, who came from Bristoe Station, and marched till two o'cock in the morning. Centreville is abandoned, and all the government property that cannot be carried is burned. The soldiers think that their winding course yesterday from the mouth of the Occoquan would measure twenty-five miles: and a few now are got into the ambulances before starting. After the artillery, teams, and all the troops have passed us, we fall in, and bring up the rear.

Friday Noon.—The whole brigade is resting in a wide, grassy plain. On the right and left are cherry trees, filled with boys picking the delicious fruit: here, are squads around little fires, (they don't burn well, for small, thick drops of rain are falling,) cooking coffee: there, are long lines of soldiers, with rubbers tied close around the neck, sitting on knapsacks, eating their dry food; and now and then you meet one asleep, all covered with his blanket. Soon the drum beats, and we are marching again. The sun is hid from us by clouds; and it is quite amusing to hear the boys conjecture the direction of the course; indeed they put it to nearly all the points of the compass. As we start off in the morning, there is much fun, and jokes fly as lively as in camp; but this grows less and less, till dark, when you hear but a little, and this seems somewhat forced. At night we pitch our tents in a mowing near a station on the Alexandria and Loudon railroad. Pickets at once are sent forward to guard all approaches to the camp.

JUNE 27.—At daybreak the bugle is blown. The rolls are called; breakfast ate; tents and blankets are rolled; and by five we are tramping. Up to nine o'clock the brigade rested three times. It seems at such halts to be the invariable custom to sit on the knapsack, or lop over on the ground, and nibble away at hard tack; but some spread their rubbers, and lie flat on their backs; and those accustomed to smoke do not now forget their old habit. At one time we made a long stop, for hundreds of teams belonging to the army of the Potomac to pass. At two we came in sight of Edward's Ferry. All around it is a beautiful, rolling country, covered with wheat and corn. Here we find many soldiers; and here we halt an hour,—during which time many wash their feet, some of them blistered and almost bleeding. We encamp for the night a few miles north of the river, expecting to start early in the morning for Harper's Ferry, or Hagerstown.

JUNE 28.—Sunday. We remained till all the troops around the ferry passed. A little before seven it is known that a chaplain is going to Poolsville and will carry letters. Now see the scribbling. Each soldier sits on his knapsack, and with a lead pencil writes a few words to his nearest friend. This perhaps is a specimen:

"MY DEAR FATHER:—I have just time to tell you that I am well, and feeling well. We have been marching three days, and are now somewhere in Maryland, near Poolsville, expecting to start in a few minutes. There are thousands of rumors, and if any of them are true, we shall have a brush with the rebels before night. Don't worry about me; for I shall come out all right, and do my duty the best I can.

Your affectionate son."

At eight we are marching,—the hottest day we have seen. Frequently you will see soldiers falling out to throw away their blankets, or all their clothing, except what they are wearing, and then run to take their place in the ranks; and at each rest, the ground is strewn with blankets, blouses and shirts. At noon we have reached the mouth of the Monocacy river. Here we halt just long enough to boil coffee and "cloy the hungry edge of appetite" with hard tack. Then we push on, rest,—on, rest again,—on,—on, no rest,—on, up a rising land. "I'd like," said the soldier by my side, "I'd like to be General just one half day, and load some of these officers with my knapsack, gun, and equipments strapped to their backs." His face is fiery red, and sweat running down it like rain on window panes; but still we push on; the front regiment has gained the height. "Halt," cries the General; and "halt" comes down the long line, repeated by the other officers. Down go the guns,—down goes everything that weighs down, and then the panting soldiers. Five minutes more, and the bugle is sounded for us to march. "The General has changed horses, we've tired out one," I hear a good natured soldier saying, as he is bending over to pick up his rifle. A mile and a half more brings us to the foot of a small mountain a little north of Adams's Station, on the Baltimore and Ohio railroad; and here we bivouac for the night. "To-morrow we are going to Antietam."

JUNE 29.—Beeves were shot and dressed last night, so we have fresh meat with hard tack for breakfast this morning. Some of the soldiers' feet are in a bad condition. I saw one round blister an inch in diameter on the bottom of the heel. "Can't go far to-morrow," said many a boy, as we closed our march yesterday. But they washed them in cold water, and all start off in far better spirits than last night, although it rains hard, and we in the ranks actually know nothing at all where we are going. We suppose the enemy somewhere in Maryland or Pennsylvania, rushing now here, now there, committing all manner of depredations. "Lee is within five miles of Baltimore and marching on the city." Last night the great battle was to come off at Antietam; and there we were going; but to-day noon, after plodding through mud and rain as fast as we can, we find ourselves at Frederick City. Here the brigade leaves ninety soldiers, unable to go farther. Some buy pies and pay fifty cents apiece, and a dollar for smallish loaves of bread. From this place we march northerly, and pitch our tents just at dark in a rich valley covered with grass, waving wheat and corn. We closed our eyes, thinking that the worst had befallen our arms, and that Harrisburg was being sacked by the rebels. We have heard that Gen. Meade is in command of the army, not knowing whether to believe it.

JUNE 30.—We commence marching at six; and halt at Lewistown in about two hours. The soldiers here buy cakes for a fair price. "Hard tack has played out, whilst green backs last," is a common remark; but on a long march it is not possible to carry soft bread. We also halt awhile at Mechanicstown. Here we find that a brigade of cavalry passed us in the night. These, too, wear out as well as infantry. I saw six sleeping in a field, whilst it was raining, and no rubbers over them. Our regiment is in the rear, and arrives at Emmettsburg just at dark; but still we must pitch our tents and have our coffee. The march this afternoon has been exceedingly hard. Two soldiers are left in houses on the way. At one time, near evening, as we had been exerting every chord for near two hours, splashing, splashing through the mud, faster, faster every moment, "it seems," said an old soldier, whose lips had never uttered a complaint before, "it seems as though the General meant to kill the whole of us." Soon one drops down in his tracks, and is thought to be dying; but stimulants are given him, and he survives, but unable to go farther. As we near the place of encampment, though not a man can hardly drag one blistered, bleeding foot after the other, I hear a few jolly fellows, as much as to say: "See here, boys, we are all right, if we have marched six days," singing: "I'm bound to be a soldier in the army of the Lord," "John Brown's knapsack," &c.; but rarely one responds, even with a smile. "I'd rather fight than stir another step," has fallen from many a lip to-day.

July 1.—Wednesday. Early we are informed that we shall not march to-day. So many lie down and sleep, and many seize the time to write home. But unexpectedly about nine o'clock orders came for us to fall in. We move on rapidly through the mud and rain, (it clears off in the afternoon,) when, suddenly, at four, the smoke, like a vast, dark, snow-drifting cloud, rolls up before us from the field of Gettysburgh, five or six miles away. Here we halt a number of minutes, and the guns are closely examined, and made sure of fire by snapping caps. From this place onward the brigade moves slower,—little talking, no straggling, each man with a sober, determined look, till a little after dark, regiment behind regiment, we stack our arms in a sloping wheat field, a few rods in the rear of the cannon now crowning Cemetery Hill, and occasionally being discharged, but not replied to. As we are approaching the field we meet women and children going back into the country, now and then looking around with terror on every face; but one middle-aged woman stands nearly still, bareheaded, whilst the brigade is passing her, screaming till she can hardly speak, "Go-a-head, boys: the rebels are off there," and swinging her large naked arms in all directions, causing general and hearty laughter among all the soldiers that see her. There is no infantry firing after we arrive on the first of July, and it is fortunate, as all are too much exhausted to endure a great deal more before rest. As soon as the arms are stacked, three men from each company are sent to fill the canteens. But no fires are kindled, and so we eat hard tack and drink cold water for supper. The Colonel comes around and says, "Every man must keep his equipments on to-night." Soon the rubber blankets are spread on the ground and we lie down, side by side, behind our guns, with the starry heavens over us, ready for any emergency; and though expecting to be roused at break of day by roaring cannon, soon, too, all are asleep.

CHAPTER XV.

JULY 2.—If the geographer should attempt to describe each square inch of the earth's surface, he would give up in despair before he had finished writing of a single country; so he wisely paints the prominent features, and leaves it for the imagination to do the rest. If I even approximate to this, and present some of the prominent features of the great battle that was fought at Gettysburg, on the 1st, the 2d and 3d of July, 1863, I shall deem myself most fortunate; but then there are the thousand displays of the bravery of nameless common soldiers as great as ever appeared in history; the thousands of bright hopes extinguished; the thousands of noble intellects destroyed; the painful wounds, the dying groans hushed by the deafening clangor of arms, and the sickening, frightful carnage,—these, these must lie concealed till the Judgment Day. If the enemy had succeeded in this battle, the whole richly cultivated country to Baltimore, Philadelphia, Harrisburg, and probably the entire

State of Pennsylvania—cutting in two the east and west—would have lain helpless at the feet of the rebel horde, to be ravaged at their will. But now the long cherished aspirations of our enemies, to invade and feed their armies in the districts of the North, are crushed forever, and the fires of war rolled back into the bosoms of those states which kindled them,—not burning, like the swift running fires that sweep over the western prairies, causing the grass to grow greener the coming spring, but rather raging with volcanic fury, it may be, in the Providence of God, to destroy, root and branch, the very institutions for which they were started.

Gen. Meade is put in command of the army of the Potomac the 28th of June. His headquarters at that time were at Frederick; Lee's north-west, across the mountain, at Hagerstown. It will be remembered that our brigade arrived at Frederick the next day at noon; but we were considerably farther south than any of the other troops, except the sixth corps, at the time the intentions of the rebel leaders were clearly known. On the 27th ult., it is estimated that forty thousand rebel soldiers, and a hundred pieces of artillery, passed through Chambersburgh, which is a little further north than Gettysburg; and there is a feasible road over the mountain between the two places. Hence the enemy, in case he should go in force to Harrisburgh, was in danger of being cut off, and also in need of Gettysburg, to proceed farther east. Not a moment is lost. They are ravaging the country,—seizing horses, cattle and all the provisions they can get. On the last day of June, the first, third and eleventh corps encamped at Emmettsburgh, and also near by were the second and twelfth. The next morning early, Gen. Reynolds, with the first corps, except our brigade, and Gen. Howard, with the eleventh, start for Gettysburgh, where they arrive a little after ten in the forenoon. The first marched directly through the town, and the enemy is soon discovered to the westward in a piece of wood, near the Theological Seminary. A portion of our artillery is got into position a half mile south of them. The great battle begins by the rebels firing first, and so sharply as to cause the batteries to commence retiring soon after; but one division of infantry goes at once to their aid,—two regiments charging on the enemy and forcing him back. The artillery is now placed further in the rear on higher ground, and this position is held the rest of the day. At this juncture, General Reynolds, with some of his staff, rides forward to learn the best place for disposing of his troops. The rebels fire upon them. The brave Reynolds falls, crying out, "Forward, for God's sake, forward!" and drops into the arms of his aid, breathing, "Good God, Wilcox, I am killed." The command of the corps now devolves upon Gen. Doubleday, who hurries up and places it to meet the charge which it is evident the foe are about to make. They advance and open fire along the whole line: but the western brigade charges upon them so rapidly as to capture six hundred prisoners. A heavy body now advances against us from the woods; they are met with volleys of lead, but are not checked till a second charge is made even more successfully than the first; but not without terrible losses to this brave corps that is battling against such odds. The eleventh corps now comes in sight; and Gen. Howard assumes command of the forces. Two charges are now made by the troops under

Ewell, but resisted; then the combined corps of Ewell and Hill,—more than sixty thousand, and outnumbering us three to one—are hurled against the tired soldiers, who have been fighting for many hours with desperation, looking, longing for reinforcements to arrive; but none come to their aid, and they are driven back inch by inch, and finally retire through the town to Cemetery Hill. It is so late in the afternoon the enemy make no other demonstrations. Here both corps are formed in line of battle; here the artillery is massed; and soon Gens. Sickles and Slocum arrive with their corps, and our own brigade. O, who can tell the feelings of those scarred heroes, weary, sweating, black with burned powder. as they saw us approaching?

Gen. Meade arrives before eleven o'clock; examines the position; and makes the following disposition of the corps:—the twelfth, commanded by Slocum, on the right; the eleventh, commanded by Howard, next; the second, commanded by Hancock, the first, by Doubleday, the third, by Sickles, in the centre; and the fifth, commanded by Sykes, on the left. The cavalry are posted on the flanks; and cannon planted to sweep every road. The line is semi-circular, and Cemetery Hill nearly in the centre of the bristling arc.

Our brigade, as I have intimated before, stacks its arms a few rods in the rear of the line of battle formed by the first corps; and expecting to be roused this morning at break of day by the enemy's guns. But no,—we lie till broad daylight, and then roll our dewy blankets and make coffee and eat our breakfast as quietly as in camp. The sun looks calmly down upon the peaceful scene,—herds grazing in the green pastures, fields of growing wheat and corn, orchards of peach and apple trees, bending under their increasing fruit, rural dwellings, and birds singing as sweetly as ever, unconscious of the awful storm that is breeding in the mysterious silence. But none will ask: "Doth dogged war bristle his angry crest?" for on the summit of Cemetery Hill, fifty cannon with their deep, black mouths, are pointing to the hills beyond the town, silently muttering defiance, and, "Don't you come this way if you want to go back;" and all along, from right to left, are many other batteries crowning the highest points: and there, too, on either side, are the thick, gracefully curved walls of gleaming bayonets.

NINE O'CLOCK.—The hundred pickets, who were sent out two hours before, from our regiment, have just come back. They have shot eight or ten rounds, and are laughing over their little exploits. The boys quickly ask them, "Did you get hit?" "Not a man." A rebel sharp-shooter climbs an oak, which has a large, bushy top, off seventy-five rods, and fires five times at Major Boynton, who is most coolly watching the movements; but soon after, the rebel tumbles out of the tree, hit by a ball from our side. About ten o'clock there is some firing among the pickets on the right and left. Our brigade is still in the wheat field,—the most lying down, and many sleeping. At eleven we are ordered up,—march a hundred rods, stack arms in a clover field, directly in the rear of the highest point of Cemetery Hill, and as before, the most lie down, many go to sleep, and a few stroll off a little way to get water, and see what they can. We are not in line of battle. Directly a brisk firing breaks out a few rods to our left, amongst the skirmishers, who approach so near each other that a number of rebel prisoners are taken. The forenoon wears away, the enemy here and there feeling our strength; and then nearly four hours of almost unbroken silence; but such silence!—such as is wont to hang over the sea, foretelling furious storms—before the iron globes begin to be hurled on their merciless errands. Now suddenly a heavy fire is opened on Cemetery Hill. The ambulances, which had been collected near, and some teams, rush back in great haste. Before it is continued a quarter of an hour, a few soldiers belonging to the eleventh corps actually run away; and half of our regiment (the other half is supporting a battery further at the right,) is ordered up nearer the brow of the hill to take their places. They move steadily the short distance, and lie down under the flying shells. For two hours now a most terrific cannonade is kept up at this point, and along to the left; for two hours the destructive missiles come, whizzing, whizzing, bursting, bursting, sending down their death-bearing pieces amongst us, and crushing through the little strip of woods to our right,—but not a soldier flinches. In the midst of the furious storm, Gen. Doubleday rides along, and says in a pathetic voice: "Boys, you will fight—won't you? The honor of your State is in your hands. This battle is to decide whether Lincoln or Davis is President."

Think not that our own artillery is inactive,—but rather sending back like destruction. Gen. Meade's headquarters are on the hill; he is calmly watching every move of the enemy. Soon comes a pause—a few moments of silence, all save the groans of the dying and the cries of the wounded—more painful than the unearthly clangor that preceded—and in a moment, long, dark lines of infantry—three columns—forty-five thousand under Hill and Longstreet, are seen moving down on our left—steadily, and seemingly irresistible as a planet in its course. The blow is most directed against the fifth corps on the extreme left; but Gen. Sickles and his brave command are not daunted at the mighty host now forming in their front. On they come, and instantly all the air is filled with the ten thousand rifle cracks, and the louder roar of artillery. "My God," says a soldier to me, "my God, if we've not got a cool brain and a big one too, to manage this affair, the nation is ruined forever."

Nearer, nearer draw the infuriated lines, and louder and louder still the infernal din of arms. "See! see! they are driving us." So it is. The third corps is being forced back, inch by inch, by more than twice their number, falling, dying, fighting with desperation—their General badly wounded in the leg,—the enemy pushing on more furiously than ever, and hurling their slaughtering volleys into our decimated ranks. The second corps goes to their aid. The contest is a little more even, but by no means equal. The rebels for awhile waver, and then spring on with increased numbers. The carnage here is terrible; but our troops stand the shock as though every man cared nothing for his life, but only to beat back the mad, raging host in his front. Gens. Hancock and Gibbon are both wounded. As our thinned lines begin to tremble considerably and show signs of giving away, the fifth corps is thrown in and more than fills up the breach. A heavy battery is wheeled on to an eminence away to the left, and sends down its destructive contents into the ranks of the enemy, shaking the hills at every discharge. For a moment, at last, the foe seemed stunned and about to stagger off before the awful tempest. But no,—through the dusky air and under the serried peaks of smoke just lifted up from the lines, behind can be seen the officers dashing along, urging on the men; and that they too are being reinforced. In a few minutes their whole columns rush on with greater force and more fury than before. The sixth corps has just arrived on the field of battle. and almost at the same instant a division from the right wing has been sent to the support of the left. All now deal such blows upon the enemy that his shattered ranks reel back, falling by hundreds at every discharge, amid loud cheers and exultant shouts of victory from our side. But it was a most critical time. Our line of battle had been broken, and the rebels dragged off a battery near the centre. Instantly the five companies of our regiment are deployed in the midst of the unabated storm of bursting shells, and thrown into the breach. We no sooner reached the spot than the Colonel's horse was shot under him and the Colonel fell. He springs up, no hat on, pistol in hand, in front, and cries: "On, boys, on." They now charge down the sloping hill, over the dead and dying, shouting, firing into the foe. After the sixth corps, the division from the right wing, and some from the first corps, were massed against them, it seemed but a moment, till the rebel lines were breaking all along and flying back in dismay. The victory is complete. Half our regiment alone recaptures four cannon, and takes two from the enemy and eighty prisoners. It became quite dark before the fighting was over at this point.

After this we go back to the brow of the hill, and much joy is expressed on account of the victory. All our wounded are taken to the field hospitals in the rear, and cared for the best they could be. A little hard tack is eaten and muddy water drank, and about ten o'clock our brigade lies down to sleep in the open field, in the front line of battle, a few rods to the left of Cemetery Hill, little dreaming that the sun would go down on a far bloodier field the next day than the last. But the enemy are not satisfied with their operations on the left, and soon after a division had been sent away from Gen. Slocum's corps, Ewell makes an attack on the right wing. And for a quarter of an hour the fight rages here, the old soldiers say, as they never saw it before. Parts of the sixth and first corps hasten to their support. The shades of night do not cool their passions, so inflamed by defeat on the left, and until half past nine, with changing fortune, the battle goes on; and to us from Cemetery Hill, in painful suspense, watching the sheets of fire streaming out from the lines through the dark but a few rods apart, each seems to send back death for death. Now our columns sway back a little, and there they stand firm as the hills in their rear, resisting every assault till ten o'clock, when the foe is completely repulsed. The din of arms soon ceases all over the field, and the weary soldiers quickly yield themselves up to sleep.

JULY 3.—Who can present a fight just as it was, waged by a hundred and seventy thousand soldiers, each determined to conquor, for sixteen hours scarcely interrupted, and often reminding one of Milton's words:

"From those deep-throated engines belch'd, whose roar
Embowel'd with outrageous noise the air,
And all her entrails tore, disgorging foul
Their devilish glut, chain'd thunderbolts and hail
Of iron globes; which on the victor host
Level'd with such impetuous fury smote
That, whom they hit, none on their feet might stand,
Though standing else as rocks, but down they fell
By thousands."

But it is a part of our history,—and let it stand a record of terror to all whom hereafter a wicked ambition may prompt to raise their hands against our government or violate our laws.

The battle commenced on the right at day-break by Gen. Slocum's troops advancing a little and delivering a heavy fire into the enemy. The soldiers under Ewell answer it with a like firing and yells, and a charge even more desperate than that of the night before. The fight bids fair to be raging along the whole line from flank to flank. We in the centre almost at the same time are awoke by the cracking of the skirmishers' rifles a little way to the left, and before we have time to pick up our blankets, and lie down between the batteries, in the front line, the hostile bombs are bursting fast and furious over our heads. For three hours now the cannonade continues at this point--we lying on our faces,—and still the savage engagement goes on to the right, not at all abated; but rather the wondrous fury that broke at once, seems much increased as more artillery is brought into play, and the musketry fire is partially drowned by their thundering peals. The combatants were soon enveloped in a pall of smoke, which hides the scene of carnage. Again and again, and again, vast columns of rebel infantry are rolled in, seeming, as it were, to the black crater of a volcano, only to be swept down in death, or swept back in disorder. The morning hours have worn away, and the sun is slowly gaining the meridian; but still on they come as if spurred by some supernatural being behind that they dreaded more than the sure death in front, till at last, as when two equal globes meet, moving with equal velocities in different directions, their shock destroys each other's momentum; so for awhile it seems here, or at least one is in cruel doubt which way the scales of victory will turn, knowing that such slaughter cannot continue long. But as the battle is growing thus fearful, reinforcements arrive, and are posted to send an enfilading fire, which quickly causes disorder in the ranks of the enemy, and soon rout, too, follows.

It is nearly noon; firing soon ceases all over the field, and the sun, which has been obscured much of the day by clouds, now shows his splendor, as if to smile on this signal triumph of the friends of liberty over slavery. It would seem that three such repulses and defeats would be sufficient to convince the foe of the futility of attempting to break through our lines. But no, before two o'clock, a hundred cannon, in a circular line, are concentrated and sending their horrid bombs on Cemetery Hill, thick as hail, and swift and crashing as thunderbolts. We have three heavy lines of battle in the centre, a few rods apart, gracefully curved as a rainbow, one behind the other. Our brigade has not moved during the day, and is in the front line, in the open field, on the left side of the hill. Here they remain for about two hours, lying on their faces, and

> "Cannon to the right of them,
> Cannon to the left of them,
> Cannon in front of them,
> Volley'd and thunder'd."

But the Light Brigade were not in quite so stormy a place as the men in the centre of Gettysburg; for our own cannon, a few feet in the rear, were vomiting smoke and burnt powder upon their backs, who lie ready to spring on the foe if he advances near. For two hours, I say, they lie there,—the shells tearing up the earth, filling the air with the splinters of trees and fences, killing and wounding many; but no stragglers go to the rear. Now they rush down the slope forty or fifty rods to the lowest spot between the contending batteries, and about midway. Here in a strip of low brush they construct a small breastwork out of an old rail fence the best they can. But the enemy saw us move and turned some of their guns upon us here and wounded a few; but most fortunate for us, the most part of their shells and grape-shot came crashing down a few feet in the rear. Soon the enemy are seen moving over the hill and forming directly in our front. They have marched but a short distance before the order comes, "Fire, Fire!" A sharp firing is continued till the rebel line wavers and diverges to our right, staggering and falling rapidly from flank to flank. No cooler, braver man, can be seen on the whole field than Gen. Stannard, who is down among his boys, to fight with them and share their fate. The front line of battle to our right did not advance when we did; so the thirteenth and sixteenth regiments are marched into the open meadow by the flank and as quickly as possible; for they are moving in a terrific storm of shell, grape and musketry. Here they change front forward, forming the new line of battle at right angle to the old, bringing them on the flank of the advancing foe, and but a few feet from them. A destructive fire is now poured into them, and before they have faced many volleys, the rebel column is broken to pieces, and the "graybacks" are throwing down their arms, running into our lines, some crying "Don't fire, don't fire!" But this is hardly accomplished before another force came charging on our left. Col. Veazey with the sixteenth is ordered back to take it upon the flank, which has been bravely met and thinned by the rapid firing of the fourteenth, under Col. Nichols. This charge is as successful as the first. Both times nearly every one of the enemy are swept into our lines; indeed I saw not one get back over the hill, so complete is the victory at this point. A short distance to the right the rebels came in three columns directly for our cannon in the front. Here the carnage was most frightful. Imagine three lines of men charging on seventy cannon as near each other as they can be managed, and then, if they are reached, thousands of soldiers ready to spring up and defend them :

> "As if the yawning hill to heaven
> A subterranean host had given."

For a moment Cemetery Hill seems but one bursting volcano, sending deadly missiles upon such frail creatures as men. The repulse is sudden and overwhelming. The next morning I visited this spot early, and their mangled dead in long lines showed how they came in triple columns. When the fighting is over at this point, our brigade takes the same position it had before the enemy appeared in their front, every now and then to receive the contents of some rebel battery in the shape of grape shot and shell. But the battle is not ended yet. Like some wild beast, mad and weakened by many wounds, and too frenzied to care for the result, they spring upon our left. First there is a heavy cannonade on both sides, and then the infantry columns sweep down the hills, and for twenty minutes the smoke and sound of musketry rise from the forest in the same places. Now the shouts from our own soldiers tell us that they are driving them. All who saw the last scene, I dare say, will never forget it. Cheers, smoke, the roar of arms making the earth itself tremble, are rolling up from the wood-covered valley; back of this, in the western sky, a dark cloud is rising, streaked with chains of lightning,—but the peals of thunder can scarce be heard, so great still is the din of battle; darkness is slowly settling down and covering the field of carnage; and away on the right, all the ridges and Cemetery Hill are covered with brave men—the weary, worn remnants of the three days' engagement—who have caught the notes of final victory from our triumphant soldiers on the left, still pursuing the foe up the hill, and answer back the cheers with cheers and shouts with shouts,—and many fairly leaping from the ground in joy and ecstacy. The great battle continued from the break of day till after dark, passing from the right to the centre, and from the centre to the left, not renewed at either point, as if the foe were too much exhausted. After the firing had wholly ceased, the soldiers of our brigade lie down with their rubber blankets over them, the most not expecting to be relieved during the night; but we are, a little after nine o'clock, and go to the rear, where we sleep sweetly till morning, though the greater part had eaten nothing during the day, and but little the night before; and could get nothing but very muddy water to drink, and not near what they wanted of this. But still I have not heard a single man complain during the two days, nor seen a murmuring lip. I, with twenty others, was left behind to see that none of the wounded, who belonged to our regiment, should remain on the field. The most of them had been taken back, after the infantry fight ended at this point, by their friends, though in great danger of being hit by shells.

It was a beautiful night; the clouds had all passed off; and the moon had risen, large and silvery bright, to shine on the bloody field, before we left. But O the cries we heard, and the sights we saw—I cannot bear to tell of these. After our own wounded had been started for the hospitals,—some on blankets, some in ambulances,—it was not yet safe to approach the enemies' lines, so their wounded lie on the field all night. I wandered back among the dead, as they fell prostrate in the fight.—the moonlight making their features more ghastly, with the words of Moore often recurring:

"And, though his life hath pass'd away
Like lightning on a stormy day,
Yet shall his death-hour leave a track
Of glory, permanent and bright,
To which the brave of after times,
The suff'ring brave, shall long look back
With proud regret,—and by its light
Watch through the hours of slavery's night
For vengeance on the oppressor's crimes."

CHAPTER XVI.

JULY 4.—Early it is reported that the enemy are retreating; but the soldiers don't know whether to believe it or not,—all hoping that it is so; for our brigade has certainly endured about all it can until it has more than one night's rest. Soldiers are sent out in little squads,—some to bury the dead that have fallen both days, and others to bring in the wounded, our own and the rebel. Now that the enemy are wounded, our boys seem just as willing to give them a drink of cold water, or something to eat, as their own comrades. This morning the soldiers of our regiment have no breakfast—some borrow a few hard tacks of other soldiers—and one soldier will always divide with another if he has half a meal himself;—but still there is not a word of complaint; for all know that our quartermaster, Nelson A. Taylor, Esq., will have rations on the grounds as soon as possible; and then the men on such occasions seem lifted up beyond their own natural selves, and to forget in a measure all bodily wants. An order is issued by Gen. Doubleday and read to each of the regiments of the brigade, that took part in the battle, thanking them "for their gallant conduct, in resisting, in the front lines, the main attack of the enemy upon this position."

The adjutant comes around to learn the names and number of those killed and wounded, that they may be telegraphed home. It is found that a quarter of my company had been hit by balls or pieces of shells, and only one killed—James Wilson, a good soldier and a fine young man.

At noon some beeves are shot and dressed; and teams have arrived with rations. Little fires are kindled all over the camp, and soon, I, with twenty others, am crowded around one of them, roasting meat—some fixing it on picked sticks, others, on ramrods bent and broken by balls flying through the air but yesterday. Citizens came to the field and offered to carry letters to the post office, of which the following may be a specimen:

GETTYSBURG, PENN., July 4, 1863.
On the Battle-field.

MY DEAR FATHER AND MOTHER:—I wrote you last when at Emmetsburg. We did not then expect to march that day: but we suddenly found ourselves tramping, and as suddenly in sight of the battle-field. When we arrived at this place, each boy's feet were very badly blistered: and all of us so tired we could hardly stand up. But the moment the cannon's smoke rose before us, it sealed every soldier's lips against complaining, and all nerved themselves to do their duty,—seeming to march easier than before. I cannot describe the battle, only to say, that for more than fourteen hours, both days, we were under fire, where shell and balls were flying thick almost every moment. We, and our friends, ought to thank God that we were not all killed, for this is really the greatest wonder. I came out of the fight without a scratch. You will have learned the names of the wounded before this can reach you. When or where we shall now move none of us know.

Your affectionate son.

We have heard but little firing to-day, and the troops around us have not been moved. Just after noon it begins to rain, and continues through the rest of the day and night. Our camp is nothing but one great mud-hole. The boys bring rails on to the ground, place them parallel, cover them with bushes, and sleep on these with their rubbers over them. We were still far too tired not to sleep soundly, although a barn stood near by, filled with the wounded enemy, whose shattered limbs the surgeons were amputating. I awoke once and heard some of them groaning, some swearing, and others praying fervently to God.

July 5.—By half past five, troops are hurrying off, we know not where, in pursuit of the rebels. After breakfast our brigade is moved a hundred rods further in front, and there remains quietly till the next morning. It is now rainy, now sunshiny, all day. A few from each company—not to be gone long—are allowed to stroll over the field, and examine where the enemy stood. All are struck with the number of their dead and the almost countless number of arms they left behind. Many of the dead are not buried yet; and in some places, where horses, caissons, guns, gun-carriages, and mangled men, are all rolled in one decaying heap, the loathsome sight and stench are hardly to be endured.

The boys are getting somewhat rested and in much better spirits than yesterday,—laughing, telling over their narrow escapes; how the balls whistled above their heads, how the shells would whir and whiz and burst, and then their white puffs of smoke gently float away in the air, and their pieces come thundering to the earth, covering them with dirt; how and where this one or that one fell fighting bravely; how two in our regiment actually ran away; how the "rebs" jumped and staggered and "tipped over" as we opened fire on them; and how the General did rightly in hurrying us the seven days that we might take part in the great battle. At night we spread our shelter tents, and sleep soundly till morning.

JULY 6.—As soon as coffee is made and breakfast eaten, we begin to march rapidly towards Emmetsburg, where we arrive before noon. We were among the last soldiers to leave Gettysburg. The most of the army was set in motion yesterday, and we learn that there was considerable skirmishing between our advance guard and the rear of Lee's army, on the day after the battle closed. Why Gen. Meade did not see fit to set us marching immediately, whether because he could not discover the exact position of the enemy, or because he knew that the army—having marched so long, so rapidly, and fought so hard,—needed a little time to rest before it could operate to advantage, I know not. But this assertion I will venture to make, namely: That when those, who think the army of the Potomac did not commence the pursuit quick enough, have fought for their country as long and as bravely as they did at Gettysburgh even, the present soldiers will volunteer to pursue the enemy, one and all; and not complain because ninety thousand veterans have not been annihilated instead of being reduced one third.

As we halted here none expected to stop but a few minutes; but we continued to remain, and just before dark pitch our tents—many have thrown them away, declaring that they would not carry even these on another seven day's march—in a piece of woods on one of the highest hills near the town. Where Lee is, and the best way of hitting him the hardest blow, are much talked of, and of course each soldier must express his opinion to his fellow comrade. There were a few rumors, such as these: "Lee has been cut off at Hagerstown?" "He is coming through this way." We got papers to day and also yesterday. the first we have seen since starting from the mouth of the Occoquan river the 25th of June. A number of thousand troops encamped near us, and considerable artillery is planted on the brow of the hill in our front. But at ten o'clock at night, when many are asleep, and the camp fires burned low, orders are sent around for each company to be up by three, and ready to start at half past three in the morning on the march.

JULY 7.—Before the bright stars have faded in the heavens, the camp fires are kindled anew. and the boys are bustling around in the forest preparing for breakfast. Soon all is ready: for our weak and wounded had been left at Gettysburg, from thence to be transported by railroad to Washington, and by daylight we are marching. Many are the places named by this and that one where we are bound; but straightway it is evident that we are going back over the same road by which we had come from Frederick. From this time onward until we make our coffee for dinner, there is hardly a moment's pause, and when there is, the boys spread their rubbers and lie down panting on their backs. Tramp, tramp, —a July forenoon is hot and long—tramp, tramp; the rumble of artillery wheels, and now and then squads of cavalry dashing by us, are about all we see or hear; and shall I not say, think of? Tramping, still tramping, sweating, chafing, puffing. "Be patient, boys; we have yet got to climb a steep, slippery, winding road over the mountain, six miles, before we pitch our tents in the Middleton valley," says the General. A while after noon we turn to the right, cross the Catochin mountain, and encamp on the west side near its foot, after it has grown quite dark. We have never seen so hard a day's march before. The citizens say that we have come more than thirty miles. "A battle must be raging somewhere, or why this rush, this steady stretch of sixteen hours' marching? and that too, by men well nigh worn down before?" With such thoughts as these the soldiers closed their eyes,—the rain spattering in their faces.

JULY 8.—Before it is fairly light we are awake, and commence marching without any breakfast, only as each nibbles a hard tack on the way. It rains violently, and the roads are all mud. So hurried is our course—one after another in the advance falling out and mixing up with those further in the rear—that in two hours you cannot distinguish one regiment from another. Near noon we halt on the top of a steep hill covered with clover, not far from Middleton Village, wet, hungry, so tired that all would most gladly lie down to sleep, expecting to continue the march in a short time. Now the clouds have departed, and the sun shines out warmly; the crystal raindrops twinkle on the green grass and leaves; and all nature smiles, and looks fresher and lovelier than before the storm had swept over her bosom. But a still greater change has come over the soldiers; for now it is known that Vicksburg has fallen; that Lee's defeat is overwhelming; and that we shall turn our faces homeward in the morning.

After the boys had eaten their dinner—the most buy warm biscuit or loaves of bread of the citizens—all go down and wash themselves in a small stream. The sixth corps is camped near us, and many from the old brigade visit their friends in ours, and congratulate them upon doing so well at Gettysburg, and upon going home. Soon the troops around us are marching towards Hagerstown. Although every man is in ecstacy at the thought of meeting his friends, yet, with pain and many regrets, did we see our brother soldiers depart, with whom we had marched so many miles and fought by their sides at Gettysburg, and always treated so kindly by them. We remain in the beautiful valley until morning. It reminded us of New England more than any other place we had seen, lying between the Catochin and South mountains, much broken, but the little hills are covered with wheat, corn, and sweet smelling clover, with pure springs of water at their bases.

July 9.—Not far from seven o'clock, we begin to march towards Frederick, where we arrive at noon. We meet the old brigade, just starting for Hagerstown, and give each regiment three as loud cheers as our tongues would let us, which they answered with cheers equally loud, and wished us a safe and pleasant journey home. The road, the whole distance, was crowded with troops—we have never seen every-body in such fine spirits—and teams to supply them, all following the retreating enemy. We march down three miles to the Junction, and there take the cars for Baltimore. Sleep and darkness soon almost unconsciously steal upon us; and by midnight we are in the latter city. It was a warm, starry night, far different from the rainy, chilly 12th of October, when we arrived here nine months before.

We remain in Baltimore till the night of the 11th. All have considerable pride to meet their friends looking as well as possible. Many—some had left their youthful mustaches to themselves for the nine months—visit the barbers' shops; and many buy new suits of clothes. We stopped here for the sick and wounded to arrive from the hospitals in Alexandria and Washington.

The next morning, Sunday, Philadelphia welcomes us back from the war not less kindly than she received us when we were going, nine months before, to defend her borders.

The middle of the afternoon finds us at Jersey city. Just at dark we go on board a steamer, but do not start out till the next morning at seven. For awhile after we had pushed off from the wharf, the deck is covered with soldiers to view the principal objects of interest; but, one by one, they go back, and in an hour the most are sleeping on the floors. At one o'clock we disembark at New Haven;—and soon those waving kerchiefs; those sweet voices; those well tilled fields; those white cottages, surrounded by flowers and fruit trees, and near by the garden patches filled with vegetables; those green pastures; school-houses and churches,—all tell us that we are once more in New England. We arrive at Brattleboro' at half past eleven P. M.; and the soldiers go to the barracks which they first entered on the last day of September before.

APPENDIX.

GENERAL ORDER—No. 68.

Headquarters Army of the Potomac,
Near Gettysburg, July 5th, 8.30 P.M.

The Commanding General, in behalf of the country, thanks the army of the Potomac for the glorious result of the recent operations. Our enemy, superior in numbers, and flushed with the pride of a successful invasion, attempted to overcome or destroy this army. Baffled and defeated, he has now withdrawn from the contest. The privations and fatigue the army has endured, and the heroic courage and gallantry it has displayed, will be matters of history to be ever remembered.

Our task is not yet accomplished, and the Commanding General looks to the army for greater efforts to drive from our soil every vestige of the presence of the invader.

It is right and proper that we should, on all suitable occasions, return our greatful thanks to the Almighty Disposer of events, that, in the goodness of His providence, He has thought to give victory to the cause of the just.

By command of Major General MEADE.

S. Williams, A. A. G.

REPORT OF BRIG. GEN. GEO. J. STANNARD, COMMANDING SECOND VT. BRIGADE.

HEADQUARTERS, 3D BRIGADE, 3D DIVISION,
1ST ARMY CORPS,
In front of Gettysburg, July 4, 1863.

P. T. Washburn, Adjutant and Inspector General:

SIR,—I have the honor to report that the Second Vermont Brigade, under my command, marched from the line of the defences of Washington upon the Occoquan, on the 25th ult., under orders to report to Major General Reynolds, commanding the 1st Army Corps.

The Brigade joined that corps at this place, on the evening of July 1st, after an exhausting march of seven days. The distance marched, averaged about eighteen miles per day. Rain fell on every day of the seven. The men marched well, with no straggling, and considering the condition of the roads, the distance travelled, from the mouth of the Occoquan to Gettysburg, could not have been accomplished in less time.

We reached the battle ground, in front of Gettysburg, too late in the day to take part in the severely contested battle of July 1st, and my tired troops upon their arrival took position in rear of the line of battle of the 1st Corps.

Before reaching the ground, the Twelfth and Fifteenth regiments were detached, by order of Gen. Reynolds, as a guard to the corps wagon train in the rear. The 15th rejoined the Brigade next morning, but was again ordered back for the same duty. about noon of that day. After the opening of the battle of the 2nd the left wing of the Thirteenth regiment, under Lieut Col. Munson, was ordered forward as support to a battery, and a company of the Sixteenth was sent out as support to the skirmishers in our front. While stationing them, Capt. A. G. Foster, Assistant Inspector General of my staff, was seriously wounded by a ball through both legs, depriving me of his valuable services for the remainder of the battle. Just before dark of the same day, our army line on the left of the centre having become broken, under a desperate charge of the enemy, my brigade was ordered up. The right wing of the 13th regiment, under command of Col. Randall, was in the advance, and upon reaching the breach in the line, was granted by Gen. Hancock, commanding upon the spot, the privilege of making effort to retake the guns of Company "C," regular battery, which had just been captured by the enemy.

This they performed in a gallant charge, in which Col. Randall's horse was shot under him. Four guns of the battery were retaken, and two rebel field-pieces, with about eighty prisoners, were captured by five companies of the 13th, in this single charge. The front line, thus re-established, was held by this brigade for twenty-six hours. At about two o'clock of the 3d inst., the enemy commenced a vigorous attack upon our position. After subjecting us, for an hour and a half, to the severest cannonade of the whole battle, from nearly one hundred guns, the enemy charged with a heavy column of infantry. The charge was aimed directly upon my command, but owing apparently to the firm front shown them, the enemy diverged midway, and came upon the line on my right. But they did not thus escape the warm reception prepared for them by the Vermonters. As soon as the change of attack became evident, I ordered a flank attack upon the enemy's column.

Forming in the open meadow in front of our line, the 13th and 16th regiments marched down in column by the flank, changed front forward, at right angle to the main line of battle of the army, bringing them in line of battle upon the flank of the charging column of the enemy, and opened a destructive fire at short range, which the enemy sustained but a very few minutes before the larger portion of them surrendered and marched in, not as conquerors, but as captives. They had hardly dropped their arms before another rebel column appeared charging upon our left. Col. Veazey of the 16th was at once ordered back to take it, in its turn, upon the flank. This was done, as successfully as before. The rebel force, already decimated by the fire of the 14th regiment, was scooped, almost en masse, into our lines. The 16th took, in this charge, the regimental colors of the 2d Florida and 8th Virginia regiments, and the battle flag of another rebel regiment.

The 16th was supported for a time in the now advanced position it occupied after the charge, by four companies of the 14th, under command of Lieut. Col. Rose.

The movements I have briefly described were executed in the open field, under a very heavy fire of shell, grape and musketry, and they were performed with the promptness and precision of battalion drill. They ended the contest on the centre, and substantially closed the battle.

Officers and men behaved like veterans, although it was, for most of them, their first battle, and I am content to leave it to the witnesses of the fight, whether or no they sustained the credit of the service, and the honor of our Green Mountain State.

That their efforts were approved by the Division General, is shown by the General Order appended to this report.

The members of my staff, Capt. Wm. H. Hill, Assistant Adjutant General, Lieut. G. W. Hooker, and Lieut. G. G. Benedict, Aides-de-Camp, Lieut. Clark, Provost Marshal, and Lieut. S. F. Prentiss, Ordnance Officer, executed all my orders with the utmost promptness, and their coolness under fire and good example contributed essentially to the success of the day.

The list of casualties appended has been prepared in haste upon the field, and is probably inaccurate in some respects. Of those set down as missing, but one is known to have been taken prisoner, and a number of them will probably appear in the lists of killed and wounded when the full returns shall have been received.

I am, General, with respect,

your obedient servant,

G. J. STANNARD,

Brig. Gen. com'd'g 3d Brigade,

3rd Divis. 1st Army Corps.

HEAD-QUARTERS 3D DIVISION, 1ST A. C.,
July 4, 1853.

General Order, No. ——.

The Major General commanding the Division desires to return his thanks to the Vermont Second Brigade, the 151st regiment Pennsylvania Volunteers, and the 20th regiment New York State Militia, for their gallant conduct in resisting, in the front line, the main attack of the enemy upon this position, after sustaining a terrific fire from 75 to 100 pieces of artillery. He congratulates them upon contributing so essentially to the glorious, and it is to be hoped, decisive, victory of yesterday.

By command of
Maj. Gen. DOUBLEDAY,
(Signed) EDWARD C. BAIRD,
Capt. and Ass't Adj't Gen.

Head-Quarters, 3d Brigade, 3d Division,
1st Army Corps,
GETTYSBURG, Penn., July 4, 1863.

"Official."
WM. H. HILL,
Ass't Adj't Gen.

HEAD-QUARTERS 3D BRIG., 2D DIV., 1ST CORPS,
Army of Potomac, July 15, 1863.

General Order, No. 10.

The Brig. General Commanding, in view of the gallantry and efficiency of the 13th, 14th and 16th Vermont Regiments, displayed at the battle of Gettysburg, directs that the flags of each of the Regiments be inscribed "Gettysburg," that the people of the State may be reminded, at the sight of these flags, of the men who bore and honored them in the hour of national danger and triumph; and that every soldier may justly be proud of his devotion to country and credit done to the State.

Nor does the General Commanding fail to appreciate the services rendered by the 12th and 15th Vermont Regiments, who, at the same time, served their country by the faithful discharge of important duties.

But while the entire command may well be proud of its laurels, they will not forget to remember the fallen dead. Let their names be embalmed in the hearts of their comrades! Let their memory be green as the sod that covers them! Let their virtues and example be a watchword in coming time! Let the tear of sympathy alleviate the sorrow of relatives and friends!

By order of

Brig. Gen. GEO. J. STANNARD.

GEO. W. HOOKER, A. A. A. G

ADJUTANT AND INSPECTOR GENERAL'S REPORT—1863.

The Twelfth, Thirteenth, Fourteenth, Fifteenth, and Sixteenth Regiments have been brigaded together, during their term of service. The brigade was commanded by Brig. Gen. Edwin H. Stoughton, until he was captured by the enemy, and was then, for some months, commanded by Col. Asa P. Blunt, of the Twelfth Regiment. Afterwards, in April, 1863, Brig. Gen. Geo. J. Stannard was assigned to the command, and continued in command until the expiration of the term of service of the regiments. Until June, the brigade was stationed in front of Washington, the different regiments being located in the vicinity of Fairfax and Wolf Run Shoals, and engaged in performing picket duty. On the 25th of June the brigade left the line, under orders to report to Maj. Gen. Reynolds, commanding the First Army Corps. The brigade joined that Corps at Gettysburgh, on the evening of July 1st, after an exhausting march of seven days, during which they marched over one hundred and twenty-five miles.

The Twelfth and Fifteenth Regiments were ordered to the rear, to protect the trains, and were not allowed an opportunity to participate in the battles of the second and third of July. On the evening of the second of July, the remaining regiments of the brigade were moved to the front line, to take the place of troops which had been broken by desperate charges of the enemy. Col. Randall, of the 13th Regiment, with five companies of his regiment, made a gallant charge, and re-took four guns of a battery, which had just been captured by the enemy, and about eighty prisoners.

The brigade held the left centre of the front line during the battle of July 3d, and endured, like veterans, the terrific fire of artillery, which was opened upon them by the enemy; and when the rebel column advanced to the charge, the Thirteenth and Sixteenth Regiments, under Colonels Randall and Veazey, changed front and attacked the advancing column in flank, performing most brilliantly the part asigned them, scattering the enemy, and taking a large number of prisoners. The Sixteenth Regiment, by another change of front, attacked in flank a second column of the rebels which was charging upon that part of the line held by the Fourteenth Regiment, under Col. Nichols, and were again successful, capturing the colors of three rebel regiments, and taking many prisoners. The officers and men of the three regiments won the most distinguised praise from all the general officers in command, and have rivalled the reputation which the "Old Brigade" has won upon many hard fought battle fields.

I annex copies of the report of Brig. Gen. Stannard and of the complimentary order of Maj. Gen. Doubleday, who commanded the division. The casualties were as follows:

Thirteenth Regiment, Killed 8, Wounded 89, Missing 26.

Fourteenth Regiment, Killed 17, Wounded 68, Missing 22.

Sixteenth Regiment, Killed 14, Wounded 89, Missing 15.

Total, Killed 39, Wounded 248, Missing 63.

Their term of service having expired, the regiments have been mustered out, as follows:—

Twelfth	Regiment,	July 14,	1863.
Thirteenth	"	" 21,	"
Fourteenth	"	" 30,	"
Fifteenth	"	August 5,	"
Sixteenth	"	" 10,	"

www.ingramcontent.com/pod-product-compliance
Lightning Source LLC
Chambersburg PA
CBHW030121030726
47498CB00007B/2497